*This book donated by*

*FRIENDS OF THE LIBRARY*

*and*

The Libri Foundation
*Eugene, Oregon*

# WILD MAN ISLAND

# BOOKS BY WILL HOBBS

Changes in Latitudes

Bearstone

Downriver

The Big Wander

Beardance

Kokopelli's Flute

Far North

Ghost Canoe

Beardream

River Thunder

Howling Hill

The Maze

Jason's Gold

Down the Yukon

# WILD MAN ISLAND

# Will Hobbs

📖 HarperCollins*Publishers*

Library of Congress Cataloging-in-Publication Data
Hobbs, Will.
  Wild Man Island / Will Hobbs.
    p.    cm.
  Summary: After fourteen-year-old Andy slips away from his kayaking group to visit the
wilderness site of his archaeologist father's death, a storm strands him on Admiralty Island,
Alaska, where he manages to survive, encounters unexpected animal and human inhabitants,
and looks for traces of the earliest prehistoric immigrants to America.
  ISBN 0-688-17473-6 — ISBN 0-06-029810-3 (lib. bdg.)
  [1. Wilderness survival—Fiction.   2. Survival—Fiction.   3. Archaeology—Fiction.
4. Caves—Fiction.   5. Newfoundland dog—Fiction.   6. Dogs—Fiction.   7. Kayaking—
Fiction.   8. Admiralty Island (Alaska)—Fiction.]  I. Title.
PZ7.H6524 Wi  2002                                 2001039818
[Fic]—dc21                                          CIP
                                              AC

Typography by Henrietta Stern

8  9  10

❖

First Edition

*to Elise Howard,*
*my wonderful editor;*

*to Barbara Fitzsimmons,*
*inspired art director;*

*and to Josh Weiss,*
*managing editor extraordinaire*

# ALASKA'S A-B-C ISLANDS
## Admiralty-Baranof-Chichagof

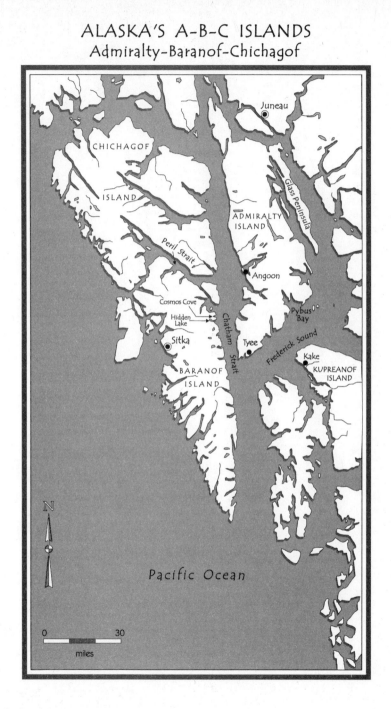

I WAS PUSHING THE LIMITS. My kayak was out in front of the others but still within shouting distance. So far they weren't calling me back.

It was the sixth day, the last full day of our trip, and this was the area where we were supposed to have the best chance of seeing the humpbacks. Gimme a whale, I thought. I'm ready for forty tons of breaching humpback whale just like on the postcards.

My eyes were locked on the horizon. The last thing I expected was action right under my nose. *Whooosh!* came a fountain of water and an explosion of breath as something huge burst out of the water only a few yards away. There, right next to me, was the head of what might have been a giant seal. Big eyes, little ears, long whiskers—I didn't know what it was. The animal looked me over for a second, snorted, then slipped back underwater.

"Wow!" I said under my breath. "Come back and give me another look, big fella."

For a minute, nothing. I was sure it was gone for good when, suddenly, the sea erupted with fountains and whooshes. This time *five* of the critters were bobbing up and down and snorting. Their large eyes were dark and mischievous. A furry water polo team with attitude, that's how they struck me.

I waved. In response, they swam straight at me. At the last second, point-blank and enormous, they slipped under my kayak.

When they popped up again, they were back where they had first appeared. Still checking me out, they snorted at me, almost comically. "Cool trick," I called.

Two, three times, I whacked my paddle on the water, hoping they would repeat their stunt so I could get another close look at them.

Same as before, they headed straight for me. Same as before, they passed right under my kayak.

"Andy!" came a voice from behind, and there was Monica, paddling toward me like there was no tomorrow. A ski racer in the winters, Monica was the trip leader even though she was the younger of our two guides. I was basically in awe of her.

"Stop! Stop!" she cried, as she reached out and grabbed hold of my kayak.

"What's wrong? I wasn't doing any—"

"Those are Steller's sea lions, Andy. They can be dangerous! They weigh close to two thousand pounds. Did they snort at you?"

"It was amazing. They wanted to play."

"Maybe," she said, raising her eyebrows, "but they can play rough. They were more like charging you, challenging you. A couple of years ago one of them tipped over a kayak. It happened to one of the other compan—"

Suddenly Monica's eyes went big, and I saw why. Not very far away, an immense whale was bursting out of the sea. Its enormous white flippers flailed as it rose twisting into the air.

For a second the whale seemed to hang suspended, water streaming off its sides. With a resounding splash, it fell on its back into the sea.

Behind us, cheers went up from the group, and someone hollered, "First whale!"

With a huge smile, Monica reached for my shoulder and gave me a forgiving pat. "Humpback whales, Andy! This is what we came for!"

With a sudden pivot, she sped toward the others.

It was going to take me a while to recover from the sting of Monica's reprimand. I was fourteen, as young as Adventure Alaska would allow on these trips, and the only kid in the group. For six days, I'd been trying so hard.

As I paddled on, I thought about what Monica had just said, that we'd come for the whales. In my case, that was only partly true.

Mostly I had come all the way from Colorado to Baranof Island to make a pilgrimage. My father had died on Baranof. Of course, Monica didn't know anything about that.

A few minutes later, with all seven kayaks paddling together, the group witnessed a second breach, and then a third. A little while after that, two humpbacks at once rocketed out of the sea.

"Okay, guys, let's quit paddling," Monica instructed. "We're about as close as we should get. Let's raft up. Grab on to the kayak next to you."

She began to tap on the hull of her kayak. "Let's let them know where we are, so they can steer clear. I'd rather not go airborne on a whale, or find myself underneath one when it falls, thank you very much."

I started tapping on my hull, and so did the paddlers in the four tandem kayaks. Our other guide, Julia, pointed excitedly to the right, where the seagulls were all worked up about something. Julia was my mother's age and our naturalist. We watched as the gulls circled, screaming, over a spot suddenly churning with fish. By the hundreds, small silvery herring were leaping out of the water, frantically it seemed, and we soon found out why. "Bubble net!" Julia cried, as four feeding humpbacks in a tight ring, jaws wide open, exploded through the surface.

I was mesmerized. My father had seen this up close, had told my mother all about it. It was on account of my father that *Alaska* had always been a magic word for me, a powerful magnet. The older I got, the more strongly I'd felt Alaska's pull.

My father had been convinced that the islands of southeast Alaska were hiding deep, dark secrets from the past. When I was five years old, he died trying to find those secrets.

Flanked by whales breaching in the strait, we paddled across the narrow mouth of Cosmos Cove. Our last campsite was in sight at the foot of the cliff. All my feelings about losing my father, growing up without him, were breaking through the surface.

Two miles. Tonight I would be two miles from Hidden Falls, the place where my father had slipped and fallen. It was less than an hour's paddle to the south.

My mother and I had thought I would come within twenty miles, not two.

When the group assembled in Sitka I'd found out that our itinerary had changed slightly, on account of the whales. When Monica said that our last camp would be at Cosmos Cove, her words hit me like a thunderbolt. I had known that name for years. It's where my father should have met the floatplane for the first leg of his journey home.

This close, I would never feel right about it unless I visited the place where my father died. I needed to get to Hidden Falls.

My mother had gone there. A year after it happened, she went to Baranof Island and Hidden Falls. She left a small carving there. My father had made it from soapstone.

For six days now, I'd been picturing myself finding that little carving of a boat and leaving a token of my own inside it. I'd whittled a tiny cedar paddle and was wearing it around my neck. If I could leave something of myself there, it would be a very good thing. I might be able to finally shake the feeling that part of me was missing.

I looked at my watch: 5:20 P.M. It was late July in Alaska, and there were hours of daylight left. The problem was, there wasn't the slightest chance Monica would let me go alone.

There was no chance, either, that Monica would let Julia go with me, or anyone else for that matter. Monica's first rule was, "The group never splits up. Never, ever." It was the first thing she'd told us back in Sitka. The second was, "The inside waters of these islands might have looked calm and protected from the airplane. Take my word for it, they are among the most dangerous in the world."

After six days, we hadn't seen any danger. Most of the time we'd been in Peril Strait, and it never looked perilous.

We paddled in formation across the cove to our last campsite. The bows of all seven kayaks hit the beach gravel at the same time, and a cheer went up. The trip was all but over. The floatplanes would pick us up in the morning.

I should have let it go. I should have figured I would find a way to get back sometime later in my life. But I'd been saving up money for a year and a half for this trip, and I knew once I got home to Colorado, Baranof Island would seem as far away as the moon.

We set up our tents along a grassy strip backed by high mossy cliffs. Along with the solo kayak, I'd drawn the one-man tent. As I pitched it, I kept my eyes on the whales. All the while, humpbacks cruised back and forth in front of camp. The tide was coming in, and the whales were breaching barely more than a stone's throw from the beach.

Suddenly it occurred to me. The tides weren't going to be right this evening. Hidden Falls might be only two miles away, but I'd be fighting the current all the way.

When *would* the tides be right? I started to do the math in my head. The answer came quickly. At first light, between two and three in the morning, that's when they'd be in my favor.

All during dinner, all during Julia's last campfire and nature talk, I couldn't stop thinking about it. It would be so easy. I could picture it clear as day, paddling to the falls alone.

L ONG AFTER THE OTHERS HAD GONE to their tents, I
stayed by the campfire. Gradually, around midnight,
the fire flickered out and the last of the sunset faded
into stars.

I lingered, listening to the explosive breath of the
whales feeding just offshore. Like steam bursting from
pipes, the sound came every few minutes from the darkness. The whales put me in a trance that stirred my
deepest undercurrents. I needed to go to Hidden Falls
like I needed air, water, or food.

I stood up, stretched, and sighed. At my tent, the
last one down the beach, I pulled off my tall rubber
boots and crawled inside. Since it was a matter of waiting only a few hours until first light, I didn't bother to
take off my thermal underwear, the heavy socks, my
wool shirt, or the outer layers of synthetic fleece—
pants, vest, and jacket. I lay on the sleeping bag with my
hands behind my head, and I asked myself out loud, "Are
you sure about this?"

The floatplanes would arrive midmorning. By noon
we would be back in Sitka. By midafternoon I'd be back
in Juneau. Twenty-four hours later, I'd be back home in

Colorado, regretting. The answer to my question was an ominous "Yes."

By two-thirty in the morning, dawn was already glowing pink and violet. The sky was mostly mare's tails. A few clouds were beginning to gather among the snow-streaked summits of Admiralty Island, the massive landmass across Chatham Strait. It looked like our group's lucky streak of blue skies was ending. Monica had kept telling us that we were getting away with murder. She was always saying that the weather could turn on a dime.

I told myself there was nothing to worry about. I was used to watching the weather in Colorado. Anything serious arrived a day or two behind high clouds.

I pulled on my rubber boots and crawled outside. My kayak was right there, safely out of reach of the high tide. I stepped into my spray skirt, cinched it around my waist, and reached for my life jacket and paddle.

Kayak at my hip, I walked around a granite boulder and down to a tiny beach that couldn't be seen from the other tents. The crunching of the gravel under my boots sounded strange, as if it wasn't me doing this.

The beach was steep; the tide was close to fully out. Careful not to slip, I eased through exposed beds of blue black mussels. Just as I had figured, I would be mostly paddling on the slack—the last hour of low tide going out and the first hour of high tide coming in. During the slack, the current is all but done flowing one direction and barely beginning to flow back the other. Paddling is easy, pretty much like paddling on a lake.

On either side of the slack, the tides ran with huge currents in and out of the straits between these islands. The currents ran as strong as the Colorado River ran back home, close to five miles an hour. For the last six days I'd been figuring it all out, how the tides made the water behave in these crazy passages, and I was certain that I understood.

My head told me this wasn't dangerous. After all, I'd paddled Ruby and Horsethief Canyons, just downriver from home, at least a dozen times. My mother, an expert kayaker, said I was ready to take on the next canyon downstream, Westwater. The rapids down there included Skull, which was hair whitewater, real serious.

My mother had a permit for both of us to paddle Westwater in September. That was saying a lot, even if the water wasn't going to be as pushy as it would have been in June.

This morning I would see only flat water. The thing was, I was a long, long way from home, and I was going to be paddling alone.

The guard hairs on the back of my neck stood up as I stepped into six inches of water, floated the kayak, then lowered myself into the cockpit. I checked my watch. It was 2:45 A.M.

No one would know I was gone. I'd be back by five-thirty at the latest. Julia and Monica would be the first to rise, around seven. "Sleep-in day," they'd announced at the end of the campfire. Everyone had cheered.

I secured my spray skirt around the rim of the cockpit, buckled my life jacket and cinched it tight.

Those guard hairs were still tingling, and now my head was telling me I shouldn't be doing this.

My heart was telling me otherwise. I started paddling, following a narrow opening through the forest of kelp skirting the shore. Then I dropped the rudder and headed south under the cliffs, keeping to the outer edge of the seaweed beds. For good or bad, I was committed.

I soon passed under Graystone Cliff. Gulls by the hundreds were screaming high above, no matter that day was barely beginning. A whir of wings over my left shoulder, and I turned to see a bald eagle flying by with a herring in each of its taloned fists. A tapping sound up ahead alerted me to a sea otter floating on its back and smashing a sea urchin against the stone it carried on its chest. Close by, another one was rafting a baby on its belly.

I didn't have a map, but I didn't really need one. I knew every place name and the shape of the coastline along these few miles by heart.

Staying close to the shore as possible, I hugged the outer edge of the kelp beds the way our group had done all week.The soaring cliffs and the mountainsides above rose straight out of the sea. The water below was the darkest shade of green, how deep I couldn't begin to guess. I remembered how close to shore the whales had fed the night before, and rapped my knuckles every few minutes on the kayak's hull. That was no pretty picture, forty tons of whale coming up underneath me.

Dawn was in full display by now, with a blanket of red cirrus flaming orange and red across the sky. "Red sky at morning," I said aloud. "Sailor, take warning."

Keep your nerve, I told myself. You're on a very brief mission.

I'd reached North Point. I could see the rocks offshore that had been indicated on the map. Once I rounded those rocks, I'd be paddling into Kasnyku Bay. I'd been making good time, incredibly good time. It was 3:15 A.M.

With firm pressure on the left pedal, I began to steer away from the safety of the kelp beds. The pedal for each foot was connected by a loop of cord to the rudder at the stern. With a river kayak, you did all the steering with your paddle, but after six days in the sea kayak I'd come to appreciate steering with my feet. It was already second nature.

In the early morning light, the glistening boulders that heaved out of the sea off North Point looked like a pod of petrified whales. We had rounded many of these rocky points during the trip. The water was always choppy out there. Clearing the rocks forced you to go a little way out into the strait, which is where you didn't want to be.

Hyperalert, I started into the open water. As I rounded the point, there was only the slightest wind and the slightest chop. Still, my breath was coming faster and my adrenaline was up. No reason to get excited—in a few minutes I had cleared the point and was gliding into the calm waters of Kasnyku Bay.

Immediately I could see the creek at the back of the bay. At the foot of a steep mountainside, it plunged out of the forest onto a strip of grassy tidal flats. I strained to spot Hidden Falls in the timber beyond, but all I could see through the trees was a hint of sheer gray cliffs.

As I paddled toward the rear of the bay, I let my mind drift across the years. My father had been hiking down from Hidden Lake with a geologist when it happened. They were making their way down the cliffs by the side of Hidden Falls.

My father had a geologist along because he was looking for a certain kind of limestone terrain called karst. Karst is known for ravines, sinkholes, underground streams, and especially for caves. My father was hoping to find caves on Baranof Island.

Their search had taken them from tidewater on the west side of the island, across its volcano-studded backbone, to tidewater on the east side. We found out later that they didn't find any caves; they didn't even find karst. Now that I'd seen for myself how the forests on these islands blanketed the bedrock underneath them, I could understand what they'd been up against.

My father, Alex Galloway, was an archeologist, a paleontologist, and a flintknapper. He was crazy about the past, especially about the migrations of human beings long before recorded history. He'd been to Africa and worked with the Leakeys, but his big passion in life was the Americas. Even when he was in college, my father had a hunch that people had been in North and South America for a whole lot longer than the experts thought.

I beached the kayak and dragged it across the flats

and up above the high tide line. I drank from my water bottle and checked the time. It was 3:31 A.M. and broad daylight. It had taken me only forty-six minutes so far. I touched the tiny cedar paddle at my neck. There was time, but I had better hurry if I was going to make it back to camp before the changing of the tide.

THE ROAR WAS IN MY EARS as I bounded up the bedrock alongside the creek. I turned a corner into cold wind and spray. There was Hidden Falls, making a spectacular plunge over the full height of the cliffs.

Two thirds of the way up, there was the narrow ledge he must have crossed so he could stand next to the plummeting water. I could picture my father resting his backpack against a tree and starting across the face of the cliff.

One little slip. One fatal mistake. His world ended, and mine and my mother's was changed forever.

Why did you have to do that? Why couldn't you play it safe, like the geologist?

My mother always said that my father was adventurous, curious, full of the joy of life: "a man whose equal comes along rarely."

Through the rainbow mist, I could see him falling. All that I really have of his voice and his eyes and the rest of him are the old home videos, not that I can bear to watch them.

For me, he never quit falling.

Falling right there at my feet. Right there.

I started crying, just weeping and bawling. Fourteen years old and crying like a baby. It hurt. It just hurt so bad. It was like the world was wringing out every organ in my body and stomping on what was left.

My eyes fell to the bedrock. There was a large dark stain on the smooth rock at my feet. I let myself imagine that it was his blood, that nine years of drenching rain hadn't washed it away.

I knelt and put my hand on the stain. I said, "I'm here."

*"Who is it?"* I could hear him asking.

"It's your son, Andy."

*"That's good,"* came his answer. *"I'm glad you came. Is your mother there too?"* I was so emotional, it didn't really feel like I was supplying his end of the conversation.

"I thought she would be, until a few months ago. Too many bills to pay. I saved up for this by sacking groceries and working at the museum."

*"Museum?"*

"There's a dinosaur museum outside of Grand Junction, just off the interstate. I'm just as interested in the past as you. I've been hanging out with the paleontologists. I've been on some digs and found a lot of fossils. At first I helped out for free. Now I get paid for giving tours on weekends, believe it or not. I got interested in paleontology because of you."

*"I'll picture you as a dinosaur hunter, then."*

"No, I'm more interested in human history. What I

want to do most is finish what you started. Find the very first Americans."

"*Ah, wouldn't that be something, Andy. But not for my sake. That wouldn't be right.*"

"For both of us," I said. "For both of us."

The *tok-tok-tok* of a raven brought me out of the spell. I began to scan the niches in the granite all around the base of the falls. Where would my mother have left the carving?

I'd heard her describe the spot; if only I could remember. There's a tree right above it, she'd said. She'd set the boat effigy on a tiny ledge she could barely reach on her tiptoes.

On the right-hand side of the falls, about fifteen feet above the bedrock, a tree had somehow taken root in the cracks. A stunted hemlock no more than eight feet tall had a foothold in the merest bit of dirt. Could that be the one?

At five foot nine, I was three inches taller than my mother. The ledge below the tree was within easy reach. I raised my hand and felt along it. Within seconds I felt the smooth touch of soapstone in my fingers.

My father's soapstone boat fit easily in one palm. It was just a simple carving of an open boat, an ancient skinboat. He had a theory that the first Americans didn't walk from Siberia, they paddled boats of sea mammal hides stretched over wooden frames.

I freed the tiny cedar canoe paddle from the rawhide loop around my neck and placed it inside the carving. I touched the little boat to my heart, then put it back on its ledge. "Good-bye," I said.

I listened for his voice but heard only the roar of the falls. I turned and ran.

At the kayak, I checked my watch. It was 4:35. I had stayed longer than I should have. The slack was over, the tide had turned. I'd have to paddle back against the current.

The first mile, in the bay, wouldn't be a problem. The second mile, along the edge of the strait, would just take me longer. Monica and Julia might even be up when I got back. I could live with that if I had to.

I began to paddle across the bay. I looked around, wondering what was different. Everything, not just the time of day, had changed a little from before.

I couldn't put my finger on it.

I felt a chill go down my spine. Halfway across the bay, the spooky tingling at the back of my neck still wasn't going away.

"You're just scaring yourself," I said aloud. The sound of the fear in my voice scared me a little more.

As I headed out of Kasnyku Bay, three harbor seals popped up and looked at me with their shy, gentle eyes. "Gotta jet," I told them as I paddled swiftly by. They slipped back under water.

I'd just left the bay and was set to round North Point when it dawned on me how still the strait was. The bay had been the same way. Eerily still. That's what was different.

I looked around. There wasn't the slightest breath of wind in the trees, not a seabird to be seen. When had there been no birds, not even gulls? No raven croaking, no eagle screaming?

It was calm, uncannily calm. This was too much of a good thing.

Outside the bay there was a strong current. It was running against me but I was making progress. I paddled on, more and more eager to get back to the group and on my way home.

Home to Colorado, I thought. Mom waiting at the airport in Grand Junction. Tell her I visited Hidden Falls. Give her the humpback whale T-shirt I'm going to buy at one of the tourist traps in Sitka or Juneau. Talk her into burgers and fries on the way to the casa. Check in with the grandparents and see if the peaches are ripe. Check my e-mail. Call Derek and find out when soccer starts. See if he wants to do a piece of the Kokopelli Trail on our mountain bikes. Call Darcy and see if she still remembers me. Ask her how she did at the horse show in Durango. Listen to the new CD I burned just before I left home. Then crash in my own bed back in good old Orchard Mesa.

All I had to do was round the long string of granite boulders that stuck out in the strait. I had to clear the point before I could get back to hugging the seaweed beds along the shore.

I pushed on my right foot pedal; the rudder at the stern responded instantly. The nose of the kayak moved right, and now I was pointed toward the farthest rock.

Once I got around that rock and could dash back to the shore, I would feel a whole lot better. The thing is, it was taking much longer than it should have because I was fighting the tide. It was just like paddling upriver, but I was strong. I could do it.

As I rounded the point, at my farthest from the shore, it struck.

Nothing I had ever seen before, not even in the canyonlands of Utah, had prepared me for wind that came on this strong and this suddenly.

One second I'd been paddling in that dead calm. Two heartbeats later I was fighting wind that was producing big swells right before my eyes.

My left foot pressed hard on the rudder pedal and I pointed the kayak toward the land. Toward safety.

Head down, I paddled hard. But now the wind was blowing violently, off Baranof Island and directly at me. Rollers were rising up right in front of me and the wind was blowing white water off their crests.

The waves were all coming toward me, sweeping away from the land. Ocean waves weren't supposed to do this. Ocean waves were supposed to come *in* to the shore.

So they aren't doing what you think they should, I told myself. Get over it.

Somehow I had to get through them.

I took a look and found the shore farther away than when I had rounded the point. I could fight the tide, but how was I going to fight this wind? No matter that I'd been paddling full bore, the land was slipping away, the wind was howling, and I was in a world of trouble.

# 4

I KEPT THE BOW POINTED TOWARD LAND, kept paddling hard, but the wind was pushing more and more waves up between me and the shore. Big rollers with wind-blown crests were running right at me.

I had to get through them, that's all there was to it. If I could reach the kelp beds, the seaweed would hold me. Julia had described sea otters wrapping themselves in seaweed to ride out a storm.

The wind was howling, just howling. Foam blew off the crests of the waves right into my eyes. The salt stung and I tried blinking my eyes clear. I kept the bow pointed into the waves and paddled as hard as I possibly could.

With my head down to avoid the spray, I broke through the top of one roller and then a second and then a third.

Was I getting anywhere? Or were the waves just passing under me? Was I any closer to shore?

I took a quick look. I didn't think so.

Head down, I paddled even harder, but the waves were relentless.

My eyes went to the shoreline again. It had to be

closer by now, but it just wasn't. I was shocked by what I saw. The shore was farther away, quite a bit farther.

Every few seconds, farther yet.

In no time at all, I'd been pushed back a hundred yards, maybe two hundred, from where I'd started. Panic nearly overwhelmed me. I pushed it back by concentrating on what I had to do.

I wasn't going to be able to keep this up. Nobody could get to shore against this wind. Nobody. How could it have struck so fast?

Now the wind was pushing the tops of the rollers so hard, they were breaking right at me and on me. I met them squarely, paddling and bracing my way through the turbulence. This was more than scary; this was going to get worse than I could handle.

I'll be all right, I told myself. As long as I keep meeting them straight on, and with some speed, I'll be all right.

If one of them turned me over, I knew there would be no righting myself. Not in a sea kayak.

My arms were starting to cramp, but I kept paddling into the waves and the wind. Getting blown into the strait was too horrendous to think about.

All the same, Baranof Island shrank even farther away.

My strength was nearly spent when it came, a wave I thought I might not be able to climb over.

*This could be it*, I thought as I paddled into the wave with all the speed I could muster.

The wave was just too tall. I couldn't climb high

enough. I felt the kayak sliding backward on the wave, and then I felt it slipping sideways. I began to feel off balance.

There was no other choice, nothing else that might save my life: I leaned into the wave, dug my paddle in deep, and held a brace long enough to recover my balance. Yet I was still sideways to the wave and in immediate danger of going over.

I knew what I had to do, and there was only the slightest moment to do it before I capsized. With a hard push on the left pedal, I dug deep with my right paddle blade and spun the rest of the way around until I was pointed toward the open strait.

I'd lost any chance of getting back to Baranof Island, but I was upright, and now I was running with the wind.

With a glance over my shoulder I saw a following roller about to catch me. I paddled with the wind and felt myself harmlessly lifted as it passed underneath me.

Now what? The wind was still blowing a gale.

There wasn't any choice. There just wasn't any choice. With the wind pushing me, all I could do was race headlong into open water.

That's where I went. Before long, I was out in the very middle of the strait, miles from either shore.

All I could do was react as fast as possible to what the water was doing. My only strategy was to stay upright, to ride with the waves in exactly the direction the wind was pushing them, and hope that the wind would blow itself out.

From out of nowhere I was surrounded by dolphins, dozens and dozens of black-and-white dolphins. They were barely off my paddle blades, under my bow and all around me, their dorsal fins knifing through the water. Some were breaching, leaping wildly out of the turbulent seas and taking a look at me before smacking on their sides into the waves. For a while they kept me company and then they disappeared.

I lost all sense of time. I was being blown down the strait between Baranof and Admiralty. On both islands, the shapes of the mountains kept changing, which meant I was moving very fast. Some time later I was much closer to Admiralty than I was to Baranof. Admiralty Island's shoreline changed by the minute. If the wind didn't let up, I would end up a long, long way from where I started.

On and on I flew. The waves kept lifting me higher and higher. In between them I ran down their faces paddling as fast as I could. In the troughs, looking up, sometimes I wondered if I could get over the top, but my kayak had so much momentum I sailed over one after the next. The wind was pushing me so hard, sometimes I hurtled over the crests off balance and had to grab a stiff brace to keep from spilling.

With all the adrenaline coursing through me, I never thought how cold the water would be if I capsized. I knew full well that I wouldn't last more than a few minutes if I spilled. As it was, I was soaked to the skin and my fingers were metal claws.

I never thought of home, never thought of the group

waking up and finding me gone. All I knew was that I was being pushed closer and closer to Admiralty's shore. Before long I would be in danger of being crushed against the rocks. For as far as I could see there were no beaches, only surf pounding the rocks and flying right up against the trees.

Ahead, the island appeared to be ending. A forested cape stuck out from the land and ended in a falling ridge, a bare, bony finger of land that was being hammered by exploding waves.

If I could stay off the shore ahead of that cape, then clear its tip, there had to be calmer water behind it. The cape should make a barrier to the wind. There should be safe water right around the corner.

Whenever it was possible, I pushed on the right pedal and pulled extra hard with my right paddle blade. I had to keep working to the right.

The shore was coming up too fast, a nightmare of rocks and white water.

I kept working. I might reach the cape. I might just reach it.

Or I might be crushed against it. A few minutes would tell. It was going to be close.

Now I was struggling with a few last strokes to clear the rocks below the tip of the cape. The recoil of a wave that had exploded against the rocks nearly tipped me. I dug a deep brace and rode it out.

Then I saw my opening, and I raced down the length of a trough between two waves. At the last moment I spun the kayak to avoid being struck sideways. I found

 25

myself in safe water. A few strokes and I was out of the brunt of the wind.

As I gasped for breath I took a quick look around. Despite the calmer water, only moderate chop, there wasn't a place to land on the inside of the cape. The shore was much too rugged. I paddled half a mile or more toward the back of a cove between the cape and another rocky peninsula.

The cove itself was studded with boulders, but it had a gravel beach at its back where I could land. That was all that counted, getting off the water and onto land.

I stopped paddling, just for a moment. There was nothing left. I closed my eyes and blew out my breath and took new air back in.

When I opened my eyes I saw heads bobbing, the huge heads of Steller's sea lions that also had taken refuge in the cove.

I saw them, and they saw me.

I started to paddle to shore. If I don't annoy them, I thought, don't even look at them, they'll leave me alone.

Ignoring them wasn't working. I heard them snorting their challenges, and from the corner of my eye I saw them plowing in my direction.

When they get close, I thought, they'll dive under me. They'll swim under the kayak.

Twenty feet away, as I was expecting, they slipped under the water. Eyes on the shore, I paddled fast. The shore was within reach.

It came as a sudden surprise—a jolt, a solid, powerful jolt under my legs. Barely able to believe it was happening, I felt myself and the kayak rising up above the water and tipping. I tried to lean, tried to use my paddle to keep my balance, but I had passed the sickening point of no return. I was going over.

Suddenly it was dark, and so cold that the sea water felt like an electric shock. I couldn't breathe and I was fighting five-alarm panic. For a split second I saw the hindquarters of the sea lion as it swam away. My hands went to the release on the spray skirt, and I began to kick my way out of the kayak.

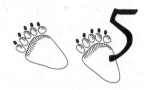

O N MY HANDS AND KNEES, I clawed my way out of the water and collapsed. The beach was black gravel and small rounded stones, driftwood sticks and seaweed and tiny beach flies buzzing in my ears. Inches from my face, a wide glassy frond of seaweed was dancing with little darts of water that splashed into my eyes. It took some grinding of my mental gears to realize it was raining.

I forced myself off my belly and sat up. I was shaking violently. The sky was dark and gray. I stared at my bare feet. My rubber boots and my socks were gone. The spray skirt was no longer around my waist. I looked at my hands, torn up from clawing at the rocks in the shallows. They didn't seem to belong to me. I could barely feel them.

As if it might help, I folded my arms across my life jacket. The shaking was getting worse. I couldn't recall the name of it, but I knew there was a name for what happened when your body got too cold. A fancy name for freezing to death.

From across the cove, a solid sheet of rain was coming right at me. All I did was stare at it.

Something came back, something from the class my mother made me take before I started kayaking. If you're still shaking and the cold is still extremely painful, there's time. It's when you aren't shaking anymore and can't feel the cold that your systems are shutting down.

The rain lashed my face. Get up, my mind screamed at my body. Do something or you're dead. Get off the beach and get out of the rain. Get in the trees. Your only chance is in the trees.

I staggered off the beach and through some grass, but driftwood logs jumbled at the back of the beach stopped me. I clambered over them and banged my leg and fell twice and picked myself up and kept going until I reached the strip of bright green alder trees and the dense bushes that grew between the beach and the forest.

The thicket of bright green might as well have been a wall. Most of it was the man-high bushes with leaves the size of small umbrellas, like on Baranof. They were wicked, I remembered, but I couldn't remember their name and couldn't remember why they were wicked.

My teeth chattered loud in my ears and the skin over my skull was so tight it felt like it was ripping. I stumbled along the front of the thicket until I found a path that led through it. The slope was slippery with the rain, and I had little control over my body. Frankenstein, I thought. I'm Frankenstein. I was shaking from head to toe. About to fall, I reached for whatever was nearest and grabbed a stalk of the bushes. My right hand came back on fire. I stopped and stared stupidly at my palm and fingers all full of tiny quills.

Then I remembered. Devil's club, that's what it was called.

My eyes returned to the trail and I saw a bizarre sight, a large bright red blob of something like jelly in the middle of the path. There were hundreds of black dots in it and I couldn't make any sense of it. I stepped over the blob and kept going.

Once in the forest, I couldn't feel the rain anymore. There wasn't much light. I was under trees as big around and tall as redwoods, a forest on an immense scale compared to what I'd seen on Baranof.

"Get your clothes off, fool," I heard myself saying. "They're wringing wet."

I sat down on a mossy log. With my trembling left hand I managed to unzip my life jacket, the fleece jacket, and the vest, then tried to make my frozen fingers undo the buttons on my wool shirt. In frustration and fear I ripped the shirt open at my neck and at the cuffs, and pulled it over my head.

With the rest of my clothes off, I sat purple-naked, shaking so hard it felt like my skinny ribs would crack, and squeezed every drop of water I could out of my clothes. I had to ignore the stinging of the spines in my fingers.

Starting with my thermal underwear, I began to put everything back on. The thermals, pants, vest, and jacket were all synthetics that weighed almost nothing and dried fast. My shirt was wool but I knew from backpacking at high altitude that wool can keep you warm even when it's wet.

Rain was dripping through the canopy of the forest, but not that much. The problem now was, the air was so cold.

Shivering and shaking, I put my life jacket back on and zipped it up, grateful for the additional layer around my chest. At least I'd had the sense, I thought, to put it on when I went paddling on flat water this morning.

It all came rushing back. It hit me full force: how totally, absolutely, monumentally stupid I had been.

Stupid, stupid, stupid.

You're a fool, I told myself. I can't believe what you did. So sure of yourself, and you knew nothing. Nothing.

I heard myself laughing out loud. My voice was herky-jerky and out of control, like my limbs. I didn't know why I was laughing. It was crazy to be laughing.

The eerie stillness of the forest immediately absorbed the sound, swallowed it up.

I tried to get warm by jogging in place. Before long I could tell it wasn't working, not nearly enough. My insides were deadly cold. Without a fire I couldn't last. I had to get some body heat back somehow. If not fire, what else? My eyes cast wildly around for possibilities. How, how?

I couldn't see an answer. I lost precious time stumbling around looking for one. All I could see was trees. The trees better be the answer, I thought. There is nothing else.

A hole in a tree? Find a tree with a hole in it and crawl into the hole?

Not warm enough. Not warm enough to pull me back.

My eyes fell on a gigantic spruce that had fallen over long ago. Its bark was gone and it was nothing but a spongy, decaying mass with ferns growing along its mossy length, farther than my eye could see.

Get inside that thing, I told myself. Somehow, get in it, or get under it, or something.

What I had in mind sounded crazy. I needed a digging tool. What? What?

A digging stick, a jabbing stick, any sort of stick.

I tore at a branch from a small downed tree. The trunk was so rotten, the branch pulled right out of its socket and I fell over backward. The branch was still sound. It had come out with a thick knot at the end that tapered down like a spearpoint. I could dig with it just the way it was.

I ran along the length of the giant spruce and found a place where it had fallen across a dip in the ground. Daylight was showing under the tree. I attacked the underside and it shredded easily. The wood was so punky it really wasn't wood anymore, just pulp. The pulp was dry, which was good, and it weighed nothing.

Insulation, I thought. Insulation might be my only chance.

I speared and dug and hacked until I had made a burrow in the underside of the rotten log. Like an animal going into hibernation, I crawled in and pulled the pulp up against myself until only my face was open to the air. I had a thick layer of dry shreds under me, and I felt like I was packed inside a cocoon. Now I could only hope that my skinny body was still producing some amount of heat. If it was, my cocoon might keep me from losing it.

If I was lucky.

It took awhile, but at last I wasn't vibrating like a power sander. Maybe the rotting tree was generating a little heat. Whatever the reason, gradually, very gradually, the shaking turned to shivering and at last even the shivering quit.

That was when I turned to worrying about what came next.

I pulled my left arm free and looked at the bombproof sports watch my mother had given me at the airport in Grand Junction. It was still spitting out numbers just fine. 3:15 P.M., July 26. What were Monica and the others doing? Were they back in Sitka, or had the windstorm and the rain kept them in Cosmos Cove? Had the floatplanes been able to pick them up?

Monica, the group, the floatplane pilots . . . it was so embarrassing to think about, I couldn't stand it. What did Monica think when she first discovered me and the kayak gone? When the windstorm struck, what did she think then?

Monica must have been sick, just sick about it. Julia too. What were the people in the group saying? My mother . . . what would she hear, and what would she think?

I couldn't believe I had done this to her. Of course she would find out, and before very long. Maybe even tonight. It would kill her, just kill her.

Maybe the floatplanes had been delayed, I thought. Maybe nobody but the group knows, even now.

There had to be a way to erase all of this, like it never happened.

The kayak! Maybe I could recover the kayak, and the paddle too. When the tides changed, the current would run in the other direction. I could paddle all the way back to Cosmos Cove, maybe even get there before a search even gets started.

I was about to start back to the beach, to look for the kayak, when a bit of motion caught my eye. Something was coming down through the forest.

It was a bear as big as a haystack, with a wide face and a prominent hump behind its shoulders.

6

THE BEAR PAUSED TO SNIFF THE AIR. My heart was jacked up full throttle, but I didn't so much as blink an eye. Time slowed to a suffocating standstill as the bear looked all around. I pictured those front claws, long as my fingers, gutting me like a trout. At last the behemoth lumbered toward the beach along the trail that passed through the devil's club.

The trail. Of course it had been a bear trail. The red jelly on the trail, that was bear scat. The hundreds of black dots in the scat, those were berry seeds.

This animal was nothing like the black bears back home. It was a dark brown and it was a walking mountain of muscle and fat. As the bear disappeared through the thicket onto the beach, I finally took a breath. I wasn't going onto the beach to look for the kayak and paddle anytime soon.

Finally I began to see straight. What an insanely stupid fantasy—rescuing myself, getting the search called off. Embarrassment was the least of my worries. Search planes were my best hope, maybe my only hope.

The problem was, would anybody even look here?

As I tried to pull bristles of devil's club from my

 35

right hand with my teeth and my fingernails, I racked my brain to remember whatever I could about Admiralty Island. Julia had pointed it out across the strait during her last campfire. Admiralty was about a hundred miles long, I remembered her saying that. It was one of the big three, along with Baranof and Chichagof. They were often called the ABC Islands.

I cast my memory back to the view from my tent. Admiralty was a uniform dark green from tidewater up to timberline. It had never been logged. The slopes of Baranof and Chichagof looked much different, like patchwork quilts. Some of the patches were dirt brown, where all the trees had recently been taken off. Admiralty's trees were old growth. Admiralty was wilderness.

Wilderness. Under the circumstances, I couldn't imagine a more ominous word, unless it was *bears*.

What else did I know about Admiralty? "All three of the ABC Islands have brown bears," Julia had said early in the trip. I knew for an awful fact that the bear I'd just seen was a monster grizzly. Brown bears, the naturalist had gone on to explain, were the same animal as grizzlies—*Ursus arctos*. Brownies, as Julia called them, got a lot bigger in southeast Alaska than the grizzlies in the interior because of all the extra protein that salmon added to their diet. Some topped a thousand pounds.

Tell me about it.

Julia said there was another name for Admiralty, the Indian name. The Indians called it the Fortress of the Bears.

I felt sick, remembering what she'd said next. "Admiralty Island has the densest population of brown bears in the world. One per square mile."

Bears went onto the beach here, I knew that already, and the beach was where I was going to have to be during daylight. An airplane wouldn't have a chance of spotting an elephant under this forest, even if it was painted orange.

Raindrops spattered around me all night, and with my mind spinning its wheels, I couldn't fall asleep. I had a raging thirst and my stomach was balled up into a stone. I hadn't eaten in more than thirty hours. When I almost felt like I could sleep, that's when the howling started.

It had come from the direction of the beach, close enough to tear out my heart and hand it to me on a plate. The howls were long drawn out and mournful, deeper pitched than the wailing of coyotes. I didn't have a shred of doubt they were coming from the throats of wolves.

A video I'd seen about wolves being brought back to Yellowstone said there was no record of a healthy wild wolf killing a human in North America. I wasn't re-assured. In the dark, that eerie howling scared me half to death. It was five A.M. before much light reached the forest floor around my hiding place. When was the soonest that rescue could come?

Today. Anytime now. Morning, afternoon, evening. If they were going to be able to spot me, I was going to have to stay on the beach.

The heavy rubber rain suit in the rear hatch of my kayak came to mind. Too bad I didn't have it, and the boots, and the hat designed to shed rain past the collar.

Knock it off, I told myself. Think about what's possible.

I should be able to find some fresh water. Maybe I could go without food a while longer, but I was going to have to find water.

At 6:30 A.M. I heard an airplane. It sounded far off, but it was sure enough an airplane. I mustered enough courage to crawl out from under my hiding place and follow the bear trail down to the beach.

The sky was leaden, and it was drizzling. I could no longer hear the airplane. No sign of the kayak. No such luck.

The beach had shrunk from what I'd seen before. What was the tide doing? Coming in, I calculated. At high tide, within a few hours, I'd be hemmed right up against the driftwood and the trees and almost impossible to spot.

Conditions were terrible for flying. A heavy blanket of clouds made a low ceiling, no more than five hundred feet judging from the slopes above. Beyond the cove, the gray face of the sea was rolling and whitecapped as far as I could see.

Would they even look for me here, on the southern foot of Admiralty?

The wind had been blowing hard from Baranof to Admiralty across Chatham Strait. Wouldn't they more likely look along Admiralty's rugged, rocky west coast, than around the corner on the southern shore?

I looked west, to the near slopes that rose jagged and sheer out of the cove and disappeared in the clouds. The climb and the descent to the west coast would be murderous without boots. At tidewater I'd come out of the forest onto a ragged strip of jumbled rocks.

Sheltered by the cape, this cove looked friendly by comparison.

Stay put, I told myself. That's what you're supposed to do if you get lost. That's what they tell hunters every fall in Colorado. You'll only make things worse if you try to hike out.

Be patient. They'll look for you here. Give it time.

I scanned the cove toward the east. Halfway around there was a break in the mountains that backed the beach. There would be a creek there, and fresh water.

Where the cove flared seaward again, almost at land's end, my eyes picked up a large rounded object at water's edge.

A whale, a beached whale. From the black-and-white pattern I recognized it as an orca, a killer whale.

There was motion around it.

I squinted. What I saw was a bear, unmistakably a bear, with two dark moving specks close by that had to be cubs. The whale was dead, and the bears were feeding off it.

In the drizzle, I stood just out of reach of the rising tide and watched the bears at the whale and the sky. The drizzle turned to rain. I should have been building some sort of shelter on the beach.

Across the cove, the bears were about to have company. Big dogs, I thought at first, but just as quickly I figured out it was the wolves I'd heard during the night.

I squinted. There seemed to be six or eight of them trotting down the beach toward the whale and the bears. They slowed to a walk, but kept coming. I wondered what would happen. The mother bear charged them, then retreated. With the cubs at her heels, she made a beeline for the trees.

With the tide coming in, I knew I had better go to the creek while there was open beach remaining. I was able to follow a thread of sand among the smooth dark beach stones and above the slippery seaweed and the mussel beds. I chose each step carefully. It would be so easy to bruise or cut my feet.

Heavy rain, in sheets off the sea, forced me into the forest before I could reach the creek. I could see the stream where it splashed across the beach after leaving a swampy estuary of muck and waist-high grass. These flats stretched half a mile or more inland before the mountains rose into the clouds.

I wrung my clothes out, then spent a couple of hours under the forest cover waiting for a break in the rain and listening for an airplane. My stomach was cramping. At the first sound of a motor, I was prepared to sprint onto the beach and wave my life jacket.

No airplanes, but miles away and barely visible through the rain, a fishing boat was passing from right to left. My spirits surged. Sooner or later, a fishing boat would pass close to shore.

# 7

IN SIGHT OF THE CREEK, I found a hole in the base of a giant spruce and crawled in for the night. My belly was full of water and nothing else. It felt like a wild animal was gnawing on my insides. With all the cramping and the shivering, the shrieking of the wind and the howling of the wolves, I had a terrible night. All the while I kept thinking about fire, wishing I could make fire. Fire to keep me warm, fire to ward off bears, fire to make smoke to signal an airplane.

Everywhere, tree limbs were draped with white, wispy stuff that looked like Spanish moss. Old-man's beard, Julia called it—some kind of lichens. Great firestarter, she said. Put a match to it and it would burst into flame. If only I *had* a match.

"Shoeless and clueless," I muttered. I wasn't even carrying a pocketknife. All I had on me, in one of the zipper pockets of my fleece vest, was a credit card in case I needed cash from an ATM. How useful.

When the light came up, I could see bears in the estuary. A mother grizzly ate grasses while her cubs wrestled. Not far away, two mostly-grown bears were playing or fighting, I couldn't tell which.

I thought about my mother, how she was counting on me. If only because they hadn't found a body, she wasn't going to count me out.

Knowing her, she was on her way to Alaska. It would kill her to wait, not to be part of it. She would try to search with the float pilots. By now she would have figured out how close I'd been to Hidden Falls. She would have told everybody to make Hidden Falls the bull's-eye of the search. Unfortunately, that wasn't going to help.

Maybe hearing about my father would help Monique and Julia understand me taking off like I did. It was awful, what I'd done to them. Right now they were thinking it was 99 percent certain I had drowned, and they would feel responsible. I wished I could say I was sorry.

I had better come through this. That was the only way I could take the weight off them, and my mother too. My mother had thought I was old enough and mature enough to make the trip to Alaska by myself.

You're a piece of work, I told myself. Good old Galloway.

From my hiding place I could see that the wolves, five gray and three black, were still on the whale carcass. There was a commotion of gulls overhead; the ravens and bald eagles waited close by. Far out on the water, a ferryboat was passing down the center of the strait.

I was just about to go onto the beach when I realized that the wolves were leaving the carcass and heading in my direction.

From the forest cover, peeking over a log, I watched them trot by in the rain—fluid, tireless, silent. They were even larger and more powerful looking than I would have guessed. Six of them passed, led by a magnificent black wolf that had to be the leader, the alpha male. A gray and a black lagged at the back of the pack. These two were more interested in play fighting than in keeping up. They stopped to nuzzle each other and to stand up on their hind legs and gnaw each other on the ears and necks.

There was something about the black one of this pair. It was a lot less streamlined than the others and somewhat bigger. It was blocky and long-haired, and looked like a Newfoundland dog.

No wonder it looks like one, I thought, it *is* one. It's not a wolf, it's a dog.

It was a male Newfoundland, a big "Newfie," as my friend Derek referred to the breed. He had one; it was half as big as their kitchen.

This one had a bright red wound on one of its ears. It was tussling with the gray wolf, a female, who had expessive facial markings and dark tips on the guard hairs of her shoulders and spine. The underside of her body, the insides of her legs, and the underside of her tail were white.

Just before the wolf pack would have disappeared in the tall grass of the estuary, the leader turned around and surprised the dog. Playing with the gray female, the Newfie had his back turned when the alpha male attacked.

For a few seconds the two were a snarling whirlwind. The Newfoundland quickly retreated. He wasn't nearly as agile as the wolf, or as powerful or aggressive. The leader drove him even farther away.

The gray wolf who'd been playing with the dog lay back her ears and howled. The dog, in return, barked at her.

All of a sudden came the sound of a motor. An airplane, and I wasn't where I needed to be.

The wolves bolted into the tall grass with the dog in pursuit.

I ran onto the beach, no matter that I was tearing up my feet. The plane was already past the cove and all I got a look at was its tail. A few seconds, then the plane was gone.

I yelled myself hoarse in rage and frustration and fear that it wouldn't come back.

From now until whenever, nothing—not rain, bears, or wolves—was going to keep me off this beach. I hastily improvised a big SOS out of driftwood.

The airplane did come back, only minutes after I'd assembled the message. I could hear it before I could see it; I had the life jacket off and ready to wave.

It was raining hard, which wasn't going to help.

At the crucial moment, I was clear out in the open, waving my life jacket, jumping up and down, and screaming. The plane roared over the cove and the cape, then disappeared to the west.

Surely they'd seen me. Surely they were about to circle around for another look.

The airplane never came back.

Maybe the pilot had been distracted for a second. Or maybe they just couldn't see me because everything I was wearing was dark blue and so was the life jacket. Through the rain, against a dark gravel beach, I just wasn't visible enough, and neither was the driftwood SOS.

It had to have been a search plane. That's what hurt the most. Exhausted, I finally went back to the forest to wring out my clothes. I tried to make fire by striking rocks together next to a bed of old-man's beard. I made sparks, but that was it.

My father would have been able to make fire. By now he would have made himself a sharp stone knife, and with the knife he would have fashioned a bow drill and made fire with it. Then he would have made himself a spear, tipped with a deadly stone point, to defend himself against the bears.

But I had never learned flintknapping, and I couldn't defend myself, and I wasn't going to be able to make a knife and a bow drill and fire.

So quit thinking about fire, I told myself. The cold isn't bad enough to kill you.

The rain was letting up. After a while, even the drizzle stopped. Where the creek left the tall grass and looped toward the beach, I went looking for fish and spied some trout. I tried to bash them with a stick. I threw stones at them. It was pointless. It was maddening.

I followed the creek down to salt water. Julia had said that all the seaweed was edible. It was everywhere around my feet, attached to individual stones by holdfasts, as she called them.

I picked out a few of the brown ones that looked like transparent brown rubber gloves and a couple of the sea lettuce. The sea lettuce was a clump of green weed with transparent blades.

"They're just algaes," Julia had said, "brown or green algaes. Even the ribbon kelp and the bull kelp is edible. You pay good money for these in health food stores."

I'd laughed along with the rest, but I wasn't laughing now. I shouldn't have waited this long.

They need to be rinsed, Julia had said. That's what I did now, in the creek.

The brown one that looked like a rubber glove tasted like one. The sea lettuce went down easier.

It all came back up.

I waited until the cramps subsided, then tried again. Chewing very slowly, I ate one clump and waited. A second clump and a third stayed down. I wondered if it would help with the weakness and the dizziness.

I had a feeling that the airplane wasn't coming back. Whatever search zone had been drawn on the map didn't include where I was, or planes would have come in the first two days. The plane that had buzzed the beach had been somebody looking beyond the search zone.

But why were they so sure the search didn't need to include Admiralty's southern coast? I racked my brain trying to think from their point of view.

Suddenly I knew the answer. They had found the kayak.

They had found the kayak, maybe even the same day it happened, and nowhere near where I was. The currents had grabbed it, and the reversing tide had sent it back to where I'd started—on Baranof. The kayak could have floated all the way back to Cosmos Cove or even farther north.

They knew that I had spilled. Spilled into forty-degree water. They thought I had drowned close to camp.

Probably they had shut down the search within a day or two. One plane, the one that flew right over me, had kept looking. My mother was probably in it.

The weather wasn't breaking up. It came on stronger than ever. I needed a shelter on the beach. What choice did I have but to keep watch? I had to believe I was going to get another chance.

Barely above the high-tide line, I drew out a square and planted poles at the corners. The poles were branches I'd broken off, each with a forked top to receive cross members that I decked with cedar fronds.

It kept raining. I sat on a chunk of driftwood under my little shelter and waited for airplanes that never came.

FOR TWO MORE DAYS I shivered in the rain and waited for rescue. I lived on seaweed, the tops of fiddle-head ferns, the few berries I could find, and one small fish that fell out of the sky. It was a herring that had slipped the grasp of an eagle.

The weather almost never let up. The clouds wreathed the tall trees with shape-shifting tendrils and shrouds. It all looked primeval, like a lost world.

The wolves seemed to have left, but not the bears. Especially when the tide was low, they came onto the beach to dig clams, to crack mussels, and to scavenge on the whale carcass.

As the bears crossed the beach, they would stand on their hind legs to get a good look at me. Every time, I was sure they were about to charge. Some of them would woof at me, but they left me alone, even the mother brownie with the two cubs. They seemed to know I wasn't a threat.

I was desperate to find something solid to eat. The mussel beds were exposed at low tide, and clams would have been easy to dig. Their siphon jets gave their exact location away.

The thing is, Julia had told us that eating wild shell-fish around here was dicey. Every so often they were carrying some kind of microscopic bugs that caused PSP, paralytic shellfish poisoning. You could never tell for sure if they were good or not. You wouldn't know until you felt a tingling around your lips and gums. By then it would be too late. Very shortly you would be paralyzed. Maybe you'd stop breathing. People died sometimes, she said, and there's no antidote.

As weakened as I was, I was thinking about taking the risk.

On my way to the creek for fresh water I discovered that the ravens were eating the mussels. I saw one tear a mussel loose, fly up high, then drop it on the rocks in front of the treeline. The raven flew down, poked the mussel, flew up with it again, dropped it a second time. This time the shell must have cracked. I saw the raven gulp down its prize.

Sudden movement on my left caught my eye. I couldn't believe it, but what I saw was all too real. From the back of the beach, for no good reason, a huge brown bear was rushing me, coming full speed. I was about to wheel around and run for the sea when I caught myself, remembering that running was the worst thing I could do.

With its ears back, the bear was pounding toward me, sand flying up all around. When it was all but on me, the bear stood up and roared. I crossed my arms in front of my face. Terror burned through me white hot and turned me to jelly.

The bear wheeled away, twenty yards maybe. It was the monster male, the first bear I'd seen on the island. He charged again, towered over me a second time, baring his teeth and flailing his claws. I was sure he was going to maul me.

For some reason he didn't. He went away mad, roaring and threatening to come back and finish the job. After that, I was through with staying put. If that bear wanted me gone, I was out of there.

How long had I been on this island—five days? I was getting weaker all the time, and help was not on the way. The fishing boats weren't going to come close enough to see me. Maybe it was too shallow, too rocky along the coast.

I had to start walking. There had to be a village, or some cabins or something, if I just kept walking.

I started east, picking my way very carefully on my stone-bruised feet, fear still buzzing in every nerve. The heavy animal musk, the stink of that bear's gut washing over me, the horrible growling weren't going to go away anytime soon. I wished I had a weapon.

Late the next day, hobbling and weak and light-headed, I came to an island-sprinkled bay that cut deep into the foot of Admiralty. The rain had stopped, but in its place fog had swallowed up the world. Only now and then, here and there, could I see anything. At one point I thought I was seeing rectangular shapes on the horizon line across the bay. Was my mind playing tricks on me?

I squinted. There really was something there. In the

foreground, a pier. Behind it, a cluster of buildings, some large, one with two tall smokestacks.

A village, maybe a cannery . . . I didn't care what it was.

Tears came to my eyes. "I'm going to make it," I heard myself say.

As I stared, the fog erased the structures, every trace of them. I had to wonder. It might have been a product of the weakness, the dizziness. Maybe I'd imagined it.

No, I told myself, it was real. I had to believe that.

On my feet, such as they were, with my overall lack of strength, it was going to take a day to round the back of the bay and find out.

When I finally did see the place up close the following day, it was all of a sudden. One moment there was nothing in the fog but trees, rocks, seaweed, and the croaking of ravens. The next moment, the village, or factory, or whatever it was materialized right before my eyes.

I stood dumbstruck. I wanted to shout for joy, but no sound came out.

The longer I stared, the more I saw that something was wrong. My heart sank. There wasn't a single boat by the pier or anywhere else for that matter, no smoke from the smokestacks, only traces of paint on the dull gray boards of building after building. I could make out the name TYEE written large across the front of one of them. Whatever this place was, it had been abandoned long ago.

No help, just ruins, just another obstacle. I was going to have to pass around the back of the pier through a welter of rusted machinery.

It occurred to me that in one of those buildings I might find some sort of map. Even if it was outdated, it would be a hundred times better than no map.

The floor of the first building was strewn with antique junk, all badly rusted: saw blades, screws and nails, outboard engine parts, and a hundred other hazards. I backed out, careful of every step I took. A rusty nail through my foot could finish me.

The next building was nearly engulfed by the forest. I stepped into a wide hallway with cubicles stacked four high on each side, beginning at waist height, on top of what looked like rows and rows of dresser drawers. The cubicles were about two feet wide, three feet high, and six feet deep. Ladders nailed to the wall down both sides of the hallway provided access.

The cubicles appeared to be some sort of storage bins. The first one I looked into was decorated with clippings from Chinese newspapers, badly yellowed over the years. Mice had pulled the stuffing out of a disgusting looking pillow.

They're sleeping bunks, it suddenly came to me. This settlement must have been a cannery, and this building must have been the housing for Chinese workers, a hideous beehive of a dormitory.

A few minutes later I was walking on a concrete floor through the biggest of the buildings. The emptiness echoed with the shrill calls of hundreds of small

 53

nesting birds that flew among the high rafters. The broad floor was empty except for several large piles of fishing nets.

Out back, I stepped into a small house with almost all its windows intact. I guessed it was where the manager of the cannery used to live.

One room of the house had an old bedstand with the wreckage of a box spring on it. The walls were plastered with faded black-and-white covers of *Life* magazine. From the early fifties, I saw as I took a closer look.

A floorboard creaked as I stepped back. A second later, I thought I heard something out in the hall—quick footsteps, it sounded like. Someone was here, in this building!

I darted into the hall and raced to my right through a room with a fireplace and bookshelves, and ran out the back door, which was open. Running away, with several books clutched in one hand and a spear in the other, was a man like a walking mountain range, a giant of a man overgrown with gray hair. His clothing, a knee-length robe cinched loosely at the waist, was made of some sort of strange fiber.

"Help!" I yelled just as loud as I possibly could.

Like a deer sometimes does, bounding away, the man held up for a second, stopped dead still, and looked back over his shoulder.

He looked startled, afraid. His eyes took me in quickly but avoided mine.

Under a pointy thatched hat, his hair was long and gray. His full gray beard reached halfway to his waist.

Over his shoulder was slung some sort of carrying bag made of hide.

"Help me!" I shouted again.

No reply, except for the croak of a raven that suddenly flew from the trees.

My eyes went to the large black bird thrashing my direction. Suddenly it ruddered with its wedge-shaped tail and swooped right at me. Its dark eyes were looking into mine. I raised my forearm to ward it off, but it pulled up at the last second. I felt the rush of wind off its wings.

By the time my eyes found the man again, he was bounding away. Agile as a fleeing buck, he disappeared into the fog and the cedars, and the raven with him.

I SNAKED MY WAY THROUGH devil's club to the spot where the man had disappeared. I looked for the slightest movement, listened for the faintest sound. Nothing. The forest had swallowed him up.

While it was still possible, I recalled every feature that I could. First off, he was big, real big: maybe six foot six, and stout as a tree trunk, but at the same time so well camouflaged he could be mistaken for native vegetation. A forest man, a wild man of the forest, that's what my head was telling me I had seen. His eyes were light-colored, probably blue, in a face that was angular and chalky gray, like an outcrop of limestone. A scar angled from his forehead to his left cheekbone. The wild man's long hair and even longer beard were so much like the lichens hanging from the nearby tree branches, they suggested that what was growing on him wasn't only hair.

His bushy eyebrows were raven black.

His robe—what had it been made of? Bark fiber, maybe, same as the pointy, conical hat designed to shed the rain.

The spear at his side was nearly his height, with a

finely crafted, fearsome-looking point. From head to toe, he looked like he had stepped out of the Stone Age.

Suddenly I was skeptical of my own senses. In the fog, I could have imagined him, every detail. Everything about the encounter and about him had been so strange, so dreamlike.

Starvation could account for it.

I stood looking at the buildings, the pier, the ruins of the cannery. I couldn't blink *them* away. In the fog, they looked otherworldly, but they were real.

An eagle flew by with a fish. A raven went *tok-tok-tok.*

I returned to the house with the *Life* covers. Still there. I went back to the room with the fireplace and the bookshelves.

The shelves were mostly empty except for a few *National Geographic*s from the 1920s and a dozen or so books that were the exact size and color of the ones I'd seen the wild man clutching in his hand. All were dusty brown. Harvard Classics, they were called. I picked one up: *Wealth of Nations*, by Adam Smith. I put it back, thinking it wouldn't have been my first choice, either.

This was absurd. A man from the Stone Age, visiting his local library. Had he really been here? How could I prove it?

Suddenly it was important to prove to myself that I wasn't going crazy. What about footprints?

Close to the spot where he had disappeared, in an opening among the devil's club, I found a single imprint in the mud. It had a woven pattern. The man must have been wearing sandals of woven thatch.

I *hadn't* imagined him. He really had been there, and I had called out to him. He had seen that I had nothing, and he'd run away.

Hey buddy, I thought, I wasn't the one with the spear.

I walked down to the water, crushed that I'd come so close to help and come away with nothing. If the wild man could read those Harvard Classics, he must have understood my cry for help.

Who in the world was he? Were there others?

An hour later I was still at the fogbound cannery. I'd searched for a map and for canned goods, any sort of food, but had come up empty. I felt so defeated. I sat on a flat rock under the wobbly pier and watched the tide rise among the barnacle-encrusted rocks. The bottom was thick with starfish and neon-green sea anemones, nothing I could eat. It was going to be difficult to make myself keep walking. It was too hard. I was too hungry.

Why hadn't Stone Age man helped me? Done something, anything?

Just then I heard it again, the thrashing of a raven's wings. I looked up and saw one of those shaggy-throated rascals eyeing me with what looked like intelligence. I had a feeling it was the same one that had been with the wild man. Did that mean that the wild man had come back?

Croaking wildly as I scrambled up the bank, the raven flew off into the forest.

The spear. There it was, just lying on the ground. Next to it lay a bone-handled knife with a stone blade. Stunned, I looked around for the wild man, but he was nowhere to be seen.

I picked up the spear. The long wooden shaft, light yet true and solid as iron, was smooth from handling. The spearhead was about four inches long and a thing of beauty. At my first close glance I knew exactly what it was—a Clovis point. My father used to make Clovis points for collectors and museums.

I couldn't believe it. This was the classic weapon of the mammoth hunters. For a long time, Clovis hunters were thought to be the first people who came to North America.

This point was a gem, elegantly chipped to sharpness on both edges and finished off with a groove down the center of each side. It was made of dark volcanic rock like the basalt in the Gunnison River country in western Colorado.

So the wild man had helped me after all. Left me the means to defend myself on the Fortress of the Bears.

The blade of the stone knife was about three inches long, and made from greenish jade-like rock. The handle was made of antler, probably deer antler. The blade was hafted to the handle with some sort of animal sinew.

Under the straps of my life jacket would be a perfect place to stow the knife.

Could I feed myself with the spear and the knife? I didn't know. If I threw the spear at something, a fish or something, I might break the point. It was too valuable to use like that. With the knife, though, I could make a long jabbing stick. The next time I crossed a stream, I would be able to spear fish. I should be able to make a lot of other things too. Enough to get by.

Then, if I followed the coast a little farther, I might get past these rocky bays. I might reach a place where fishing boats hugged the coast. Signal one fishing boat and all this would be over.

I had to keep walking, but walking was already too hard, too painful with the bruises and all the small cuts on my feet. As soon as I thought about it some more, my gratitude to the wild man wore thin. I couldn't eat the spear or the knife. He could have invited me to dinner.

I laughed out loud. This was all too crazy to be believed.

At least you can still laugh, I told myself. That must be a good sign. I tried the knife on a lock of my hair. It was sharp as a razor.

Make something to protect your feet, Andy. Weave some sort of sandals like the wild man's.

Out of what?

The answer came immediately: cedar. Julia had said that the Indians had been able to stay warm on this rain coast for thousands of years because of their mastery of the inner bark of the cedar tree. The wild man must have mastered it too.

When I got started again I was wearing footgear of sorts. I'd figured out what inner cedar bark was, freed a slab of it with the knife, made strips, pounded them soft with a rock, and woven a crude pair of sandals. They were two layers thick, so they would last. It had taken me the rest of the day and half of the next. They looked awful, lashed over the tops of my feet and around my ankles, but they would do the job.

I'd also made a long jabbing stick with a sharp wooden point. All I needed now was a salmon stream, and I wouldn't be hungry again. Sushi would suit me just fine.

I followed the coast to the east. From far off came the sound of a foghorn. A ferry, I guessed. I thought about the cafeteria on that boat. Unbelievable amounts of food. Hot food, hot showers. People to talk to. Cell phones. But mostly, food.

Midafternoon, the fog finally started to lift. There was another creek up ahead, the biggest yet. In Colorado it might have been called a river. As I hurried toward it I pictured salmon so thick I could walk across on their backs. That's what I really needed, a salmon run.

What I found was a few trout that flashed away into the holes under the banks. With a groan, I lay down on my belly and made myself drink some water. Nothing on this island was ever going to be easy.

Where the creek crossed the beach, I rinsed seaweed. Bite by bite, I put a disgusting amount of it into my stomach. Why weren't there salmon in the stream, big fat salmon, so many I could spear any one I wanted? I was sick of this, so sick of the hunger, like a wolverine in my insides, and it never went away. I didn't know how much longer I could stand it. Most of all, I was sick of my luck.

My eyes fell on a bed of mussels. I grimaced at the image running through my head: I was starving to death in the middle of a grocery store.

Every so often they're poisonous, Julia had said.

*Every so often*, I thought. As in, *once in a while*. As in, *rarely*. It was just that they were risky.

I was ready to take that risk. If chances are good that they're edible, I heard myself thinking, I'm going to try it. I can't be unlucky *all* the time.

A minute later I was smashing a mussel with a rock, prying away pieces of shell with the knife. It wasn't like I'd made a conscious decision. It was just knowing that people eat mussels in restaurants from coast to coast, and imagining myself being lucky for once.

I would eat just one, nibble it at first, see what happened. If I felt that tingling sensation Julia talked about, I would quit.

Out of its shell, the mussel was about as long as my little finger and slimy like a raw oyster. I couldn't afford to slide the whole thing down my throat. I had to be careful.

I chewed slowly. No tingling sensation, no numbness. It was tough going. Maybe after the first few I would pound them with a rock to soften them up like I did with the cedar bark.

I chewed the whole thing up and swallowed it. I ate a second one.

It was when I was chewing the third one that I felt

the tingling. Just a little tingling on my tongue and along my gums and the inside of my lips.

As fast as I could, I spit the slimy stuff out. I tried to retch what was already in my stomach but I was unsuccessful. I stuck my finger way down in my throat, again and again—that didn't work either. I wondered if the poison was numbing my senses, like the shot you get before an operation.

Suddenly, everything felt strange. My vision started to swim, and I felt myself losing my balance. Fearing the worst, I grabbed the spear and the knife and dragged myself off the beach so the rising tide wouldn't drown me.

Before I could get to tree cover, I was struck down. Just struck down like falling timber.

# 10

WHEN I CAME TO, darkness engulfed me. It took a while before I figured out I was looking up at the sky. I could see stars and the ragged edge of a cloud bank lit by moonlight. Other than flat on my back, I had no idea where I was.

The faint lapping of surf jogged my memory. I remembered the mussels, the tingling, the numbness, and I remembered running.

I tried to roll over but I couldn't move, not at all. There was no sensation in my legs or my arms. I tried to curl my fingers into a ball but I felt nothing. Nothing at all.

Blink, I told myself.

I couldn't. The word came to me, the word that would describe what had happened. Paralyzed. I was completely paralyzed.

It began to drizzle. The rain fell into my open eyes.

I knew that I must be breathing, maybe just enough to stay alive, but I couldn't hear my breathing. I could hear the surf and the birds, I could see the sky, and I could think. That was all.

My mind was on my mother. Anytime now, my

breathing could shut off completely. Then I would die, I would simply die.

In case that was going to happen, I had to concentrate on my mother. I willed myself to think only of her. After she lost my father it was just the two of us, and now she was going to lose me. Forgive me, I thought. I am so, so sorry.

I must have blacked out and fallen into dreams. I was with my father, and he was teaching me flintknapping. I was using an antler tip to fleck small chips from a spearpoint. It was already fluted down the center on both sides; we were making a Clovis point.

Suddenly I saw that he had changed. He had long gray hair and a long gray beard. "You look different," I said, and he replied, "Well, you know, I've been dead a long time."

None of this quite made sense, but I was happy just to be with him.

"Would you like to go on a journey with me?" he asked.

"You know I would," I said, "but I should let Mom know I'm going to be gone."

"Oh, I'm not so sure you can do that."

"Why not?"

"Because it's against the rules. I'm under a certain set of rules here. I have to go on the journey, but if you want to stay, I will understand."

"No," I said desperately, "I want to go with you."

My father grabbed up the spear we'd just made. Somehow, when I wasn't looking, he'd attached the point to a long wooden shaft. I was disappointed that I'd missed him doing the hafting. "Let's get going," he said.

Across rivers and over mountains I followed him, along the seashore and over higher mountains. Everywhere there were bears, monstrous grizzly bears. They would stand on their hind legs and they would lay back their ears and woof at us, but they never charged.

"Why don't they ever charge you?" I asked.

"They know they can't touch me," he replied.

"Because of your spear?"

"Because I'm dead. Bears are very intelligent. They know."

We kept going until he led me to a certain mountainside. "You can't tell because of all the trees," he said, "but that entire ridge is karst."

"Limestone?" I said. "The kind that makes caves?"

With a wink, my father replied, "Just might be," and then he led me up the mountainside to a small opening in a knobby gray rock formation.

"A cave?" I asked.

In reply, he reached inside and brought out two helmets, each with a headlamp.

I asked, "Does this mean you've found the earliest Americans?"

"Not yet," he said.

We went inside. The formations were exquisite beyond belief. My father led me on and on, until we came to an abyss. We were looking into the depths of an immense well that seemed to have no bottom.

"Look," I said, "across from us, the cave keeps going

on the other side. It might be possible to keep going on that ledge that swings around the side. Have you been beyond here?"

"It's against the rules."

"But why?"

"*You* can go. It looks perfectly safe. I'll wait right here."

I aimed my headlamp for a better look. The ledge was ridiculously narrow, and water was seeping across it. "Forget I ever mentioned it," I said.

My father didn't say anything. Obviously, he wanted me to try it. The next thing I knew, I was starting across the ledge. I got to the part that was wet and slippery. It was no wider than a balance beam, and was angled down toward the abyss. "I don't know," I muttered. I looked over my shoulder. My father waved me on impatiently.

All at once I was slipping, slipping and falling. I reached out for a grip but my hands found only slick white stone and I pitched head over heels into the abyss.

Now I was in free flight, falling, falling, falling . . .

Suddenly everything changed. I was on my back again and looking straight up into the face of a bear. It was right above me, broad and huge, silhouetted against the stars. I could hear it sniffing me, I could smell its breath.

I wasn't dreaming. Being with my father had been a dream. The bear was not a dream. I'm conscious again, I thought. I've come to, and the bear is real. I'm still lying here paralyzed, and the bear is real.

The bear's face pulled away and stars replaced it. The clouds have cleared, I thought. Maybe they're gone for good. At the edge of my vision, I saw the bear's claws. The bear was still there. Gently, it was raking the life jacket that protected my chest.

I tried to feel my fingers. Still no response. The bear was gone. I willed myself not to black out.

I couldn't prevent it. Now I was on a raging river and paddling for my life. The walls of the canyon bristled black and narrow. Higher up and stepped back, they glowed a vivid red orange. This was Westwater Canyon, I realized. How many times have I heard my mother talk about it?

I looked over my shoulder for her but she wasn't there. I didn't understand it. She was always right behind me.

The whitewater was getting worse, and the river was full of rocks—jagged teeth, sleepers, and submerged stones that should have been deep enough for me to slide over. Somehow they weren't. At the stern of my kayak, something was hitting the rocks. My rudder, I realized.

I looked over my shoulder and there was my mother. "That sea kayak isn't right for this river," she told me. "That's why river kayaks don't have rudders."

A roar downstream brought my head around. The river was taking a plunge down an impossible-looking set of whitewater stairs. And at the bottom of the stairs, the river smashed up against the black cliffs.

"What's the deal?" I yelled back.

"Skull Rapid!" my mother exclaimed. "That's Skull down there—right down there at that screaming left-hand turn."

"I didn't have any idea it was going to be this bad."

"You can do it," she shouted. "Just watch out for the Room of Doom. It's in a pocket you can't see down there next to the wall. If you're too far right, the water off the wall will throw you into the Room. Got that?"

"But I'm in a sea kayak!" I tried to yell. My words were lost in the fury of the moment. It was all I could do to stay upright. Down the stairs I went, through mountains of exploding whitewater. At every moment, I thought I was about to spill, but somehow, miraculously, I was keeping my balance. The black wall was flying by on my right; I caught a glimpse of the Room of Doom. It was a whirlpool with no escape, like they always talked about. A dead cow was swirling around and around.

I looked back upstream. Where was my mother? I looked downstream. Where was she?

She just wasn't anywhere. The river had swallowed her up. All I could see was screaming birds where my mother should have been.

I couldn't bear any more. I heaved and struggled and fought my way back to consciousness.

There was a bird on my chest. A seagull. Dawn had come and a seagull was leaning into my face. It had a red spot on the side of its bill. The gull had a predatory look to it, as if it was just about to stab me with its beak.

That's exactly what it was about to do. Stab me in the eye.

Birds do that, I thought. It thinks I'm dead. The first thing it will go for is my eyes.

I struggled. I struggled just to close my eyelids. I couldn't. I could hear other gulls screaming and now I could see them flying in from all sides.

A second gull landed on me. The first one turned around and attacked it. I could hear their squawking and the beating of their wings, but I was powerless to do a thing.

One of them was back in my face.

I heard a loud bark. A deep, loud bark—two, three times. The bark of a dog?

The gulls flew off screaming as the face of a dog appeared directly above mine. It was a very large dog with a broad head, a large, long-haired, black dog. Dried blood caked one of its ears. I had seen this dog before.

Derek's Newfie? I wondered.

Then I remembered. This was the Newfoundland that had been running with the wolves.

The dog licked my face two, three times. Its tongue was wet and scratchy.

Don't leave, I pleaded mentally. Don't leave, or the gulls will peck my eyes out.

I waited, hoping the dog's face would reappear.

It did. The dog sniffed me like the bear had sniffed me, and it licked me again.

The dog left my vision. I couldn't tell if it was staying

or if it had gone away. I was afraid it had gone. Its face didn't come back.

Yet neither did the seagulls.

A while later I thought I heard a snuffle close by, and still later I thought I heard a yawn. I prayed that the dog was lying close beside me. Had stayed with me.

At last I could move my eyelids. It was then I realized that I could breathe deeper. I could feel my fingers, I could feel my toes.

Eventually I could move my head to the side. No dog, only forest and mountains against a bright blue sky. I rolled my head to the other side, and there was the Newfoundland lying in the sunlight next to the spear.

"Good dog." I mouthed. Little sound, if any, came out.

In response, the Newfoundland beat his great tail up and down.

I reached my right hand toward him. He smelled it, and then he licked it. The dog placed his great paw over the spear, and then he nuzzled the spear.

I understood immediately. He was with me because of the spear, because I had that spear.

As I INSPECTED THE DOG'S EAR, he nuzzled the spear shaft. It was six in the morning, and the sun was already climbing high in the sky. It was warm. Finally it was warm again.

The fur on the Newfoundland's ear was matted with blood and dirt. Flies were pestering his ear and the back of his head. If I could clean the fur, I could get a look at the wound.

I tried to stand, to move over to the creek, but dizziness knocked me down. The dog got up and stood next to me. With a hand on his great back, I steadied myself and stood up.

Something made me glance upstream. A bear was sauntering by.

The Newfoundland, sniffing the wind, looked directly at the bear. The dog didn't seem concerned. I snatched up the spear.

The bear gave us a wide berth. It crossed the stream and angled toward the beach. I steadied myself on the spear and hobbled to the creek bank.

It felt good to splash water on my face and in my

hair. I took a long drink, raked my hair with my fingers, then sat on the bank as the dog waded into the water. He turned around and snapped at the flies bothering his neck.

I closed my eyelids and aimed them at the sun. I hadn't felt this warm since Baranof Island.

The dog waded back and allowed me to rinse his ear. The cut wasn't that bad. But where my hand rested on his neck, I felt a thicker mat of bloodied fur and discovered a wound that was more serious. "You run with a rough crowd," I told him. My voice came out as ragged as I felt.

The Newfie nuzzled my hand and wagged his tail. I was amazed that a dog capable of holding his own with wolves was this docile toward me. I wondered if the man with the spear was the only person this dog had ever known.

The man with the spear, I wondered. Who in the world is he?

Suddenly I was trying to sort out one of those crazy mixed-up dreams of a few hours before, when I lay paralyzed. My father and I had been making a spearpoint together. Suddenly he was all different. He had long gray hair and a big beard, and he was much older.

Though it didn't occur to me then, it did now: As my father led me into the cave, he looked just like the wild man. What was that all about?

I knew the answer. Deep down, since I first laid eyes on him, I must have been hoping that somehow the wild

 73

man and my father were one and the same. That all this time, my father had been alive and hiding out on this island.

Nice try, I thought. If my father had ever been missing, there might be reason for hope, but his body had been recovered at the foot of Hidden Falls.

I shook the painful cobwebs out and returned to the present, to the dog. As I rinsed and cleaned the neck wound, I had to keep chasing the flies away. The wound was a couple inches long, nasty enough that a vet would have closed it. The best I would be able to do, now that the wound was clean, was to wrap something around his neck to keep the flies off.

My thermal underwear top was extra long. I wouldn't miss four inches.

I stripped to the waist and still I felt warm. The sun had burned a large blue hole in the sky. The clouds had shrunk to the east, far beyond the cliffs that rose out of the sea in the foreground.

Starting at those cliffs, I couldn't walk the coast. What was I going to do now?

For the time being at least, I had a companion. I didn't feel nearly so gloomy as I had before I'd eaten the mussels. For some reason, my stomach wasn't cramping anymore. Maybe this was just a side effect of the poison.

I sliced the material from my thermals, rinsed it thoroughly, then tied it around the dog's neck. For the time being, the flies couldn't get to the wound.

The wind was starting to blow. It was nine in the morning. A new blanket of ribbed clouds was racing in from the west. The sunshine wasn't going to last. I took a quick bath in the stream.

The dog suddenly became agitated. He started trotting off, barking at me. No doubt about it, he was telling me he was leaving. It seemed for all the world like he wanted me to follow. He kept trotting up the stream bank, as if he intended to follow the stream inland.

As I pulled on my clothes, I had one eye on the dog and the other on the cliffs. "I'm not sure if I should go or stay," I called to the dog. "I'm finally close to deep water. Next to those cliffs, maybe I could flag a fishing boat."

With an air of finality, the Newfoundland walked far up the stream. He looked back only as he was about to disappear behind some brush. Again, he barked.

He was waiting, but he wasn't going to wait long. I had to make a decision.

The dog, somehow, was my only lifeline. Everything else was uncertain. My only certainty was this dog. He was in prime condition. He knew how to find food of some kind, and was bound to lead me to it.

Unless his food was provided by the wild man.

If that's where he leads me, I thought, then so be it.

I pulled on my life jacket, tucked the knife away, and snatched up the spear.

# 12

THE NEWFOUNDLAND WAS FLANKING the broad, swampy meadow, keeping to the high ground along the edge of the forest. I was following in a daze. It was a struggle to keep up. The poisoning sickness, on the heels of starvation, had left me weaker than ever.

On my right, suddenly, a small miracle: a bank of salmonberry vines speckled with bright red fruit. There were blueberries, too, everywhere I looked.

There was bear sign here, tracks and scat, but at the moment no bears. I leaned the spear against a tree and picked berries as fast as my hands could move. They were indescribably sweet.

Not too fast, I thought dully. See if your stomach will accept them.

I slowed down, but even so, they all came back up. The nausea hit me hard; I couldn't keep my feet. After a few minutes, I thought, I'll try again.

The dog came to my side, sat on his haunches. I followed his gaze. The sea of emerald green grass and bushes on the estuary below rippled like sails in the wind. The Newfoundland was watching a mother brown bear and three cubs. They were following the creek toward salt water. He lost interest and began to nose around for something to eat.

I thought my stomach was ready for another try. This time it accepted the fruit. I kept eating.

I had to laugh, remembering that Julia had told us that nearly every blueberry has a little larva inside. "There's a certain fly that lays its eggs in the blueberries," she explained. This, after the group had gorged to the gills on one of her nature walks. "Perfectly harmless," she assured us with a mischievous smile. "Good protein."

"Good protein," I said to the dog, who turned from gumming old deer droppings to lapping fresh bear scat, the kind that looked like a pile of red jelly. I recalled how I'd been counting on this dog to lead me to food. Maybe that wasn't such a smart idea.

I felt a small surge of strength as the fruit sugars coursed into my blood.

It was comforting, recalling Julia's face. On account of her calm manner and her love of natural history, she had reminded me of my mother. It came as a jolt when I realized that I could only half remember Julia's face and Monica's too, and the faces of the other people on the sea kayak trip. It seemed like I'd known them in another lifetime.

The Newfoundland was impatient to be underway. I followed. Soon the easy going ended. We climbed a high ridge that appeared to be a spur of the island's mountain backbone. Mercifully for me, the dog was following deer trails that angled up the slopes. A couple of times

I had to retie loose, flapping ends from my makeshift footgear.

On the far side of the ridge, under deep timber, we dropped several thousand feet. At last, through the trees, I saw the slope bottoming out at a rushing creek. The creek was crisscrossed by deadfall spruce and hemlock.

The Newfoundland seemed eager to get down there. I soon understood why. The stream was teeming with sockeye salmon. "This is more like it," I told him.

I approached cautiously. To my relief, there wasn't a bear in sight. The dog waded into the shallows, lunged at a couple of fish making furious runs around his legs, and missed. He soon came up with a big salmon thrashing in his jaws. The Newfie waded out of the shallows, then dropped the salmon and pinned it with one paw, just like a bear. The body of the fish was bright red, its head dark green. The dog began to strip the skin down the fish's side, exposing the bright red meat.

With an occasional look in my direction, the Newfoundland ate the flesh from the backbone. Rather than flip the fish over and eat the other side, he waded back into the stream for a new one.

By this time I'd whittled a sharp point on a stick of alder and waded into the stream. In a couple of minutes I had my own salmon. For mercy's sake, I quickly severed its spinal cord behind the neck. The big fish thrashed a few times from reflex, then lay still.

I sliced a fillet from the backbone on each side and washed them in the stream. I sat on a log in a patch of sunshine, draped one fillet over a branch at arm's reach, and began to eat the other one, stripping the red meat with my teeth from its backing of skin. The meat was more than tolerable, and my stomach was going to accept it.

I had just finished the first fillet and was about to reach for the second. A bit of motion caught my eye. I looked up, and there was a big bear at streamside, not forty feet away. Over the rush of the creek, I hadn't heard it approach, not at all. Why hadn't the dog barked?

The Newfoundland, rather than barking or running away, was slowly moving *toward* the bear.

For its part, the bear had its head to the ground. It was standing over the spear. Why hadn't I kept the spear at hand?

The knife was also out of reach, there on the gravel where I'd used it.

Wagging his tail, the dog waded the stream and walked right up to the bear. To my amazement, the Newfoundland rose on hind legs and pawed the bear's shoulder. In response, the bear gently raked the dog's side with its claws, then took the dog's entire head in its jaws.

All the while, the brownie had his eyes on me. I kept looking from the bear to the knife. It was too far away.

Anyway, it was too late. The bear was ambling over to me. To me or the fillet on the branch, I couldn't tell.

The bear stood on two legs and clawed the air. I stayed exactly where I was and tried to calm my jack-hammering heart.

The bear came down on all fours, approached the last few steps. With one eye on me, the bear reached out and flicked the fillet from the branch, then proceeded to eat it practically at my feet. I could have almost touched the huge muscled hump on its back.

There was a scrap of fish left under that giant paw. And here was the Newfoundland, nosing in as if to take it for himself.

The bear growled at the dog, and the dog backed away.

It was all so strange, so dreamlike, and I couldn't begin to understand what was going on.

When the bear was finished eating, he turned around and planted himself at the foot of the log right next to me. Just sat there on his hind end and put his huge face next to mine.

I didn't know what to do. I did nothing. I tried to keep as calm as I could.

The bear got up, nuzzled the dog again, then ambled away.

Hours later, as I followed the dog up the flank of another mountain ridge and deeper into the island's interior, I was still trying to sort out what had happened, and how, and why.

I got nowhere. I had no idea.

It was dusk by the time an explanation came to mind. The big Newfoundland and I were holed up next to each other in a soft pocket among the trunks of giant spruce trees, and I was drifting off to sleep. There's only one way to explain it, I thought: It never happened.

Maybe I was still paralyzed, still back at the beach. Maybe everything since was dreams, too.

My hand went to the dog at my side. I stroked the long black fur. The dog lifted his broad head and licked my hand.

I felt like I was conscious. Right now, it didn't feel like dreaming. But was I actually here, under this forest, with this dog?

Before I found any answers, I was asleep. I was so exhausted, and so confused.

M ORNING BROUGHT RAIN, cold, hunger, and reality. I
hurt too much for all of this not to be real.

Deeper and deeper into the wilderness, the dog led
me on. We climbed out of the forests and onto mountain
meadows where it was higher and colder and there was
no shelter from the rain.

The Newfoundland led me higher yet onto the short-
grass tundra, alongside an ominous bear highway of
deep, alternating footwells filling with water. Rain
clouds were hanging on the snowfields and peaks
above. My feet hurt a lot; my sandals were only two
notches more comfortable than torture devices. I was
getting slammed by a tidal wave of doubts. Maybe I'd
chosen dead wrong to follow the dog. Going inland was
looking like the last thing I should have done.

I had lost all my markers. There was a spear in
my hand and I was following a huge black dog through
the clouds. Everything familiar was gone: home, my
mother, my grandparents, my friends, Orchard Mesa,
Grand Junction, the heat, the Colorado River . . . all
gone, replaced by the numbing immensity of this dreamlike island.

The Newfoundland had been pausing to sniff the wind and for some reason, was quickening his pace. Through the drizzle, near the foot of a massive landslide scar, a red mass of some kind was heaped on the tundra barely above the tree line. I was so cold I couldn't begin to guess what it was.

The dog suddenly halted, perked up his ears, listened intently. Then he tilted his head and began to bark, each bark coming slower than the previous one and the last trailing into a sort of howl.

A little closer and I could make out large black birds on and around the red object. Ravens. Then I made out the glint of bone. The ravens were on some sort of carcass. A bear, of course—nothing else was that big. But why no fur?

The dog approached cautiously, and so did I. The drizzle wasn't strong enough to mask the droning of flies or the smell of all that meat gone rancid. I was shocked by how much the skinned-out animal resembled a human being.

In the soft spots around the carcass I made out the imprints of boot lugs, three different patterns. Three hunters had stood here, I thought dully. I'd missed them, missed the chance to get off the island with them. I was a couple days late, but close didn't count. It might as well have been a year since they'd been here.

The bear's skull was missing. Why was that? Two gaping wounds marked the exits of high-powered slugs from the chest cavity. The birds had opened up the belly and dragged the guts out onto the ground. The redness of it all, the rawness, was even more shocking up close. There wasn't a trace of the hide; the paws and claws were missing. All four feet had been sawed off.

What kind of hunters would do such a thing? Poachers? Maybe it was a good thing I hadn't come across them. A witness to the crime, that's what I would have been, and who knows what they would have done with me.

I backed away. The Newfoundland was tearing away meat along the backbone, growling all the while at the ravens hopping close to the carcass. An eagle was watching regally, biding its time from a spruce at the edge of the forest. I noticed dog tracks even bigger than the Newfoundland's. No, they were wolf tracks. The wolves had been here, but judging from the carcass, they hadn't eaten. Why not?

When the dog had eaten his fill he led me back into the forest and down to another salmon stream. It was teeming with sockeyes but the Newfoundland didn't pay them any mind. He splashed through the stream and started up the slope on the other side. I tried to get him to stay with me while I made another jabbing stick, but he was leaving whether I came along or not.

Freezing cold, I followed. Cursing under my breath, I started up the beginning of a steep slope that was a patchwork of giant trees, knobby gray outcrops, and sheer cliffs. Where in the world was he going?

Behind a massive spruce that had fallen against the cliff, the Newfoundland trotted up a steep ledge. He looked back for a second; I tried to call him back but he kept going. I had to scratch my way up on all fours. I followed along narrowing ledges that zigzagged upward a hundred feet or more above the valley floor.

All at once there was nowhere to go. We were standing above thin air. It was fifty or more feet straight down to the beginnings of a steep talus slope.

I was at my wit's end—frustrated, freezing, exasperated. For no apparent reason, the dog was all excited, as if he'd reached his destination.

Immediately ahead of us along the cliff, the rain was dripping from the outer edge of big overhang and a long, shallow cave underneath it. It wasn't a true cave; it was more of a big rock shelter. An alcove was what we would call it in the Southwest. It was in nearly inaccessible alcoves like this that the ancient Indians had built their cliff dwellings in the red cliffs back home.

The dog was acting like he had to get into the alcove. I was losing all patience. We were separated from the floor of the alcove by seven or eight feet of thin air. Even with dry footing I couldn't make a leap like that, not from a standing start, and neither could he.

Now he was standing up against the trunk of a cedar that grew out of the ledge and leaned high over the gap. Barking and wagging his tail, the Newfie was acting like there was something up the tree. I hoisted myself up on the rocks for a look.

What I found was a small coil of rope on the shoulder of the first branch. The rope was tied to a jagged outcrop above. Soon I was back down on the ledge with the free end. It was braided from inner cedar bark, and obviously sturdy. Meant for swinging across to the alcove, to a food cache if I had at least one lucky bone in my body.

The dog was going crazy, and I was nearly as excited. "Okay, okay," I said. "I'm hungrier than you are." I swung across and landed easily on the floor of the alcove.

A few steps toward the interior of the alcove, and I could see that it was a good forty feet deep and twice that long. Another step, and my eyes took in more surprises than my brain could begin to process: a stone cooking hearth, a beautiful long table of polished cedar planks, a huge chair made from hide stretched over a bone frame, maybe whalebone.

I went straight to the hearth. I put my hand to the ashes in the fire pit. No hope of reviving them: they were as cold as I was. A large bowl carved from stone, with a big cedar spoon inside, had been left beside the fire pit. On all sides, there were prehistoric implements: mortar and pestle, a stone slab and grinding stone, baskets of many sizes, wooden storage boxes, a stone ax leaning against a neat stack of firewood. Close at hand was an ample supply of tinder including a bin full of old-man's beard.

"Anybody home?" I called. The only reply was my echo. Next to the kitchen, neatly arranged on hand-crafted shelves, were dozens and dozens of Harvard Classics and *National Geographics*.

The guard hairs on the back of my neck stood up. The alcove was full of hiding places. What if the wild man was here, right now, watching me?

Back at the ledge, the dog was barking. How was I supposed to get him across?

Everywhere my eyes fell, I found neatly arranged artifacts. Everything seemed to be made of wood, stone, sinew, shell, or bone: axes, mauls, scrapers, fish hooks, line, rope, bags, fishing nets, knives, spears, clubs, bows and arrows, atlatl darts, enough points to arm a clan of cavemen, the components of a bow drill for making fire.

Why would anyone live like this? Talk about survivalists. The guy must think the end of the world is at hand. He could be seriously on the run from the law, but what kind of criminal would go to all this trouble?

The front of the cave was shielded from outside view by the dense tops of towering spruces rooted on the slope far below. With a glance above me, I discovered a wooden ramp, well out of reach, that was drawn up against the underside of one of the branches. It was held by a rope that ran through a couple of pulleys carved from wood. The rope was tied off a few paces away to a branch at shoulder height. I lowered the ramp and the dog came bounding across.

Something to eat, there had to be something to eat. Fortunately, there was. I discovered all sorts of dried food stored in cleverly made cedar boxes: smoked salmon, venison jerky, mushrooms, vegetables, and herbs I couldn't begin to identify. One box was filled to the top with small cakes made of berries, fat, and shreds of dried meat. Pemmican, that's what they were. Drinking water was funneled from a collecting trough at the outer edge of the roof into storage in large wooden boxes.

The smoked salmon was delicious beyond belief. I wolfed the jerky and washed it down with water. The pemmican cakes were more filling than mincemeat pie, and the berries made them sweet. I fed the dog but he didn't have nearly my appetite. It was all so filling I finally had to lay off. I was bloated.

Food in my belly warmed me some, but I was still shivering. I thought about trying to make a fire with the bow drill but I had a good idea how difficult that would be.

At the back of the alcove was a wooden bed, knee-high and cleverly constructed without a nail or screw. The mattress, under an outer layer of sewn-together hides, was stuffed with something firm yet comfortable. In cedar boxes close by I found handmade clothing, some of it leather and some woven from cedar bark. When I came across a pair of sandals—works of art compared to mine and a whole lot softer—I quickly tried them on. The fit was sloppy but good enough when I lashed them tight.

In another cedar box I discovered a bearskin sleeping bag, with the hide to the inside and the fur to the outside. I would sleep by the hearth, not in the bed. It might help if he caught me here. For a few hours I would have a roof over my head. At first light I'd stuff a hide bag with food, sling it over my shoulder, and keep marching.

Toward the far end of the alcove I came across the

spot where the wild man must have made his points. Lithics were everywhere, flakes and larger fragments of stone. I was so young when my father died, I don't have many memories, but I remember him chipping on stones, making arrowheads. I used to play at it alongside him, as close as he would let me get, knocking one stone against another. Sometimes the stones would break, and I would think I was getting somewhere.

An array of harpoons leaned against the back of the alcove. Some were lightweight, with points of bone and shell, some were heavy, with points of stone and barbs made from the tips of antlers. Next to them was a small stack of club-like devices. They were bulky at one end with wrappings of bark that had been slathered with pitch. Torches.

Standing there, I thought I heard a continuous rush of wind, and close by. This was odd; there wasn't any wind in the trees.

I walked toward the source of the wind and discovered a crevice in the back of the alcove, a dark, jagged opening, man-high. Another step and I realized that the wind was rushing out through the crevice. The wind was coming from *inside* the mountain.

I moved in front of the opening. The wind was surprisingly strong. I knew what this was. This was how Lechuguilla, the famous cave in New Mexico, had been discovered.

This was a cave, the real thing. These cliffs must be karst limestone. This was the entrance to a cave! In fact, it looked a whole lot like the entrance to one of the half dozen caves my mother and I had been into with a caving club in Missouri the summer before.

The torches, I thought. The wild man must use them inside. Why does he go in there and what has he found? It was all too much to think about.

I had to rest. Across the fire pit from the dog, I stripped and bedded down in the bearskin bag. Free of my wet clothes, I was warm soon enough. In the gathering darkness I closed my eyes. I was torn between fear and a strange sense of peace. I pulled the bearskin bag over my shoulders, thinking about my mother and how she would tuck me in when I was little.

For now, at least, I was safe and warm. And I was at the entrance of a cave the likes of which my father had died trying to find.

# 14

I AWOKE TO A WILD WIND SWAYING the branches that shielded the alcove. My watch said it was four in the morning. I looked around for the dog, but he was gone. I hadn't thought to pull the drawbridge up.

Get out of here, I told myself. Now, while you still can. Anyone who would live like this, you don't want to meet up close. Some variety of crazy. Get up, get going, find some real help, get home.

I snatched up one of his hide bags and stocked it with food, enough for a week if I made it last.

I was about to go when something caught my attention. The low morning light, through a sudden break in the clouds, was shining into the alcove at an angle that bounced it off the ceiling and lit some kind of pattern on the back wall.

My eyes were drawn to a pair of finger-length curves. Man-made carvings? In a flash of recognition I saw tusks on a mammoth, a woolly mammoth standing on its hind legs. I stepped closer, astounded, only to make out hunters surrounding the mammoth, hunters with spears. My hand reached out and touched. What an exquisite sculpture, all in relief, in limestone. All polished, all perfect.

I took a step back and realized there was more,

much more: saber-toothed cats, giant bison and bears, ground sloths . . . it went on and on.

Another step back, and I could see that all the figures were carved within a much larger pattern . . . a map of the Americas, but noticeably different from our modern map.

I looked closely at Alaska, high above me on the wall, almost at the ceiling. Alaska was still connected to Asia.

Then I knew. This map was of the Americas during the Ice Age, when sea level was down, way down, and Alaska was connected by land to Siberia. I was looking at the famous land bridge! Walking large across that bridge was a band of hunters: men with spears, women with tumplines across their foreheads connected to baskets on their backs, the head of a baby sticking out of one of the baskets. I could see in a flash that these were the Clovis people, named after the first discovery of their spearpoints near Clovis, New Mexico.

The figures on the land bridge were heading for a deep furrow in the smooth limestone—the famous corridor through the ice sheet, the corridor that led south through interior Canada. As they emerged from the ice, in the heart of what is now the United States, that's where the hunters were attacking the mammoth.

True enough, I thought, but that's not the whole story. It's a shame that all the archeology buffs, like the crazy Michelangelo who made this, are so stuck on the land bridge. It's all that they know.

The more I looked, the more I saw. Here was the Mississippi River, the Missouri, the Colorado. . . . There was the Grand Canyon, and there were the mountain ranges: the Appalachians, the Rocky Mountains, the Sierras. Incredible.

My eyes scanned farther south, and I recognized the pyramids of the Aztecs and the Maya, a city on a mountain in South America that had to be Incan. Maybe it was Machu Picchu.

The light on the mural was dimming as clouds raced over the sun. I heard a rustle, like the sound of wings, close by in the alcove. I turned, expecting to see a bird. What I found was a giant of a man standing right next to me, little more than an arm's length away.

I was so startled I could have dropped dead. I was looking up and into the cold eyes of the wild man himself. The scar running from forehead to cheekbone was fierce enough, but not as terrifying as his eyes, staring and pale and bloodshot. "What are you doing here?" he demanded.

His voice was gravelly and powerful. It reverberated like a mountain storm, like thunder. I reeled backward, barely keeping my feet.

"Your dog. . ." I began. I was in shock. I hadn't heard him approaching, not at all.

The wild man was trembling, a mountain about to explode. I looked away; his raven was hopping around the hearth picking up bits of food I had dropped. "Your dog led me here," I managed to say.

In his bark clothes and cone-shaped hat, the wild man towered over me. With his long gray hair and beard, his sheer size and musky animal smell, he was a nightmare up close. His hands were as big as hams, and his forearms were like fenceposts. Even his face was muscled, taut and tense as a pulled bowstring. He dismissed my answer without a word; it was all in the lift of his bristling black eyebrows and the suspicion in his pale blue eyes.

"Really," I insisted. "I think it was because I had your spear. Your dog recognized the spear. But when you weren't here, he left."

The wild man wasn't listening. Those eyes were staring at me with an mix of confusion, disbelief, and hostility. They went to the spear at the hearth, the one he'd left for me at the cannery. "Nobody has ever found this place before," he said slowly. "Nobody."

"I'm sorry," I began. He raised his huge mitt of a hand, flecked with small scars, and cut me off.

"How long?" the wild man demanded. His hoarse voice hit me like a club.

"How long what?"

"Since the dog was here."

"Only a few hours, I guess."

The wild man didn't say another word. He snatched up his spear and started toward the drawbridge.

I was thinking I'd give him five minutes, then I'd clear out. This guy was beyond spooky. I was relieved he hadn't mentioned the bag over my shoulder or looked into it.

As he was leaving, he grabbed the rope that controlled the drawbridge. He walked across the drawbridge with the rope in his hand. At the far side, he started pulling on it.

The drawbridge started going up; it could be operated from either side. He was cutting me off, trapping me in the alcove!

I ran to the edge. The drawbridge was already high above me, and the wild man was securing the rope to the tree that grew from the other side. He was also tying off the rope I had used to swing into the alcove. I yelled, "Hey! What do you think you're doing?"

He looked at me, said nothing. He wasn't going to waste the words.

The raven flew to his shoulder, settled its wings, and squawked at me. With that the wild man turned his back and started down the ledges toward the creek.

"Hey!" I yelled after him. "You can't do this!"

I heard nothing in return. I didn't shout again. I had to think. I had to figure out what was going on.

"Nobody has ever found this place before"—that's what he had said. What he meant was, he had a big, big problem now, and it was me.

The man had to be a fugitive, a very successful fugitive for a long time. He must have committed some awful crime. I should have taken that possibility more seriously. I'd turned his world upside down.

First, he was going to tend to his dog. Then he was going to deal with me.

How could he solve his problem, when *I* was the problem? If he pushed me off the cliff, or used one of his weapons on me, who would ever know?

No one. No one even knew I was on this island.

He was as cornered as I was. He was going to have

to do something about me. Waiting for him to come back would be suicide.

I judged the leap it would take to reach the ledge on the other side. It just wasn't possible.

I was frantic to get out of there. I leaned over the cliff looking for a way down. There were hardly any handholds, and it was a sickeningly far drop.

Tear his table apart and make a gangplank? The boards weren't long enough, not nearly. Shinny down the trees that shielded the alcove? Impossible. The last forty feet there weren't any branches, and the trunks were too big around to hang on to.

What about *climbing*? I thought desperately. I could climb to the limb that the drawbridge was suspended from. It might be possible to belly past the drawbridge and out onto the skinny end of the limb where it rested against the top branches of the tree on the other side.

I eyeballed it again. It was way risky, not a bit like climbing the apple trees in the orchard back home.

*The cave.* It came to me like a bolt from the blue: the cave was the answer. There was too much air moving through the entrance for it to be sealed. There had to be another opening.

If I could make fire with the wild man's bow drill, I could use his torches.

I was caught between the devil and the deep blue sea. Climbing the tree was the devil. Going into the cave was the deep blue sea.

Now, choose.

# 15

WHAT WAS I DOING WRONG? I had the bowstring looped around the spindle, I was sawing back and forth with the bow. It was agony, and it was taking forever. The spindle was creating plenty of friction, but all I could manage was a thin plume of smoke. I could only hope that the wild man wasn't finding his dog and wouldn't find him anytime soon.

The base of the spindle squeaked as it drilled continuously in the socket. Heated sawdust was building up around the base of the spindle and turning black. Smoke kept rising, the cedar was smouldering—so why couldn't I make flame?

Too much breath, maybe. Too much desperation. Gently, Andy, gently.

I had seen a bow drill demonstration once at the Museum of Natural History in Denver. It had looked so easy.

It wasn't.

At last a tiny coal glowed orange and stayed orange. I gave it breath while feeding it old-man's beard, not so much as to smother it, just enough to give it fuel and opportunity.

At last, a fragile wink of flame.

More old man's beard, but gently.

Finally, fire.

With my free hand I reached for a torch, then brought its head close to the flame. That was all it took. The torch sputtered at first, then fingers of flame ran around and around it until the entire pitchy head was ablaze.

I threw the carrying strap of the hide bag over my neck and shoulder. In addition to the food, it had room for two spare torches. With a glance over my shoulder I started inside the cave. The wind nearly blew out the torch but it stayed lit. This is crazy, I thought, but I kept going.

The entrance passage was a long slide of loose rock. I took it sitting down. Water dripped from the ceiling. At the bottom of the slope was a large room lit with dim natural light. I stopped breathing when I saw dozens of bones and skulls. The wild man's sandals had left marks here and there. I jumped to a grisly conclusion, and my heart started jackhammering.

With the torch a little closer, I saw that the skulls weren't human after all. They were bear skulls. A few twists and turns, and I left behind the twilight zone, as cavers call the first stretch of dim natural light. From now on I would be totally blind if my torch failed. At the slightest hint it might go out, I'd light another one.

I followed the passage, always downhill, into caverns draped with stalactites, countless numbers of them hanging from the ceiling, and rows upon rows of organ pipes. They all dripped water. There wasn't any wind that I could feel. I reassured myself that cave air slows almost to a standstill in big rooms. There had to be another opening.

The air was cold, but I was dressed in all my layers, and the pitch in the torch burned hot and kept me warm enough.

I walked around blue pools on smooth white flow-stone terraces made of calcite, the mineral that forms from water percolating through limestone. Standing back from the pools was a forest of stalagmites ranging in size from baseball bats to the columns of a Roman ruin.

I entered a room bigger than the atrium inside the Hilton Hotel in Grand Junction. It was just as high and a lot wider. From the ceiling high above hung enormous white mineral chandeliers. The walls were encrusted with draperies of flowing stone, fragile bush-like mineral growths, soda straws, and delicate strands of angel hair.

My torch was still burning bright. It might last a long time. Only if I had to light the third one was I going to turn around.

The cavern almost pinched closed. To keep going I had to duckwalk under a low ceiling streaked with black from the wild man's torches, then scramble over a series of boulders.

I came into another great room with six emerald pools, like jewels in a necklace, strung the length of its floor. I threaded my way among them. The walls were decorated with stone corals, some ribbed like radiators and some dimpled like brain coral. The pools were deep as some of the deepest hot pools in Yellowstone, and so clear I could see smooth white rocks, like giant cave pearls, glittering on the bottom.

I entered a maze, a series of passages that wound around and over and through one another like tunnels in an anthill. At one point my eyes were on some strange feathery crystals on the ceiling. When I looked down again to the floor, it wasn't a moment too soon. I was two steps from the edge of an abyss.

The pit was circular, an immense well, uncannily like the abyss in the dream I had when I was paralyzed. The torchlight barely reached the other side.

Carefully, I sat close to the edge but not too close. I leaned forward with the torch but couldn't see the bottom. The light was just swallowed up. My stomach swooned with the falling sensation from the dream.

I got to my feet and carefully made my way around the abyss along a flowstone ledge that was wider than the one in the dream, but not by much. After that the cavern narrowed and pitched downward. I passed a place off to the right where wind was whistling through a small, jagged opening not much bigger than a rabbit hole. It might have been big enough to squeeze through. The wind indicated much more cave, and the strong possibility of a way out in that direction, but it would be a worm crawl for as far as I could see into it. No, thank you; I would stick with this cavern, where I could stay on my feet.

My torch was dimming. Most of its head was gone. I lit the next one. It flamed bright and I kept going.

A minute later I came to a chamber with a long, narrow pool that, strangely, had ripples on its surface. How could that be?

I wet my fingers in the pool, then tasted my fingertips. It was salt water.

I shaded my eyes and made out a strip of faint natural light in the distance. Here was what I had been looking for, an exit, but I'd never expected it to open onto the sea. My spirits crashed. This entrance was useless. I wouldn't survive swimming out of the cave in forty-degree water.

My torchlight fell on an unnatural-looking object perched on the highest of the calcite terraces to my left. I climbed up to have a look. I was taken completely by surprise when I discovered a boat, a boat with a paddle. No, two paddles—there was even a spare.

Thank you, wild man. Finally, a break.

Here was a skinboat just like the ancient people used, made of hides pieced together over a wood frame. It was as long as a large canoe but twice as wide across the beam, just the right size to squeeze out of the cave— at low tide, that is. At high tide, the entrance would be underwater.

Was this why the wild man used the cave? To get to his boat? A boat stored where it couldn't possibly be discovered?

I tossed the hide bag inside. "I'm out of here," I heard myself say, and the echoes said it three more times. I propped the torch where it would keep burning and dragged the boat down the terraces to the water. I climbed in and paddled for the exit.

As I approached the jagged opening, the water got rough, so rough the boat struck the rocks as it was jostled from side to side. The wind had been blowing hard that morning, and now there must be a storm raging outside.

Maybe this isn't so smart, I thought, as swells surged through the opening and pushed me back. The tide was coming in, and I had only so much time before the opening closed. As it was, I was going to have to duck if a swell lifted me up. What I really needed was a helmet, or to have arrived here an hour earlier.

Suddenly the water level dropped—a trough between swells—and I shot out of the cave into the open air, clawing at the last with my hands. I ducked my head and began to paddle as a swell lifted me up and almost tossed me back against the rocks.

Through sheets of rain I could make out tall cliffs on both sides. I was at the back of a V, a shallow V in the cliffs that provided almost no shelter from the gale. The sky was purple black and the strait was all whitecaps and waves breaking toward me. This skinboat would capsize out there, no doubt about it.

No hope. No chance. For the time being it was all I could do to keep off the cliffs. I had to get back inside the cave, and quick.

I managed to get the boat turned around and pointed back toward the cave. The entrance was looking awfully small. I didn't know if I was going to be able to wedge back through it.

In between waves, I rushed the entrance. The bow bounced off one side and I stroked hard, twice, and got it aimed inside. A wave pushed me sideways. I paddled hard on the other side and got it pointed inside again. A wave lifted me up and suddenly I was higher than the entrance and being pushed right into the cliff. I fell onto my back, or my head would have been crushed.

The boat was wedged inside the opening and was taking a beating. I got up on my knees, tried to claw with my hands, and succeeded only in bashing the top of my skull as a swell rose from underneath.

Whether it was my doing or the weather pushing from the outside, I squeaked into the cave. The top of my head was pounding. I touched it gently and my fingers came back bloody.

Somehow I had banged my right shoulder as well. Great, just great.

Back where I'd started, I dragged myself out of the boat, retrieved the burning torch, sat down. All I could feel was pain, the deep, dull pounding of my skull and the wrenching ache in my shoulder.

What now? Drag the boat above the high-tide line and wait for low tide to come back?

Well, that's what I was going to have to do. Wait for hours and pray for the weather to calm down.

I waited. Time dragged so slowly it was torture. Seconds were like minutes, an hour felt like a day. My second torch was dimming when I spied light flickering off the walls back in the cavern. My breath caught short and my heart skipped a beat. As I rose to my feet I saw the silhouette of the wild man coming down through the cavern, holding a torch aloft. He was moving quickly.

I had to do something quick, and suddenly I knew what it was. I grabbed up the bag and ran in the wild man's direction. The rabbit hole I'd passed was near. I might be able to squeeze my skinny hips through that tiny opening if I was very lucky.

Suddenly every depression in the Swiss-cheese wall on my left looked like my rabbit hole. I wasn't going to find it in a panic. I had to get myself under control. The wind, I remembered, had made a sound rushing through it. I closed my eyes and heard a faint whistle. The rabbit hole was still ahead of me.

As soon as I got there, I shoved the bag and my life jacket through. A glance over my shoulder, and I saw the wild man closing in on me, almost running. He could see what I was about to do. There was something different about him. . . . He'd exchanged his bark clothing for leather.

Too bad, I thought—I could have lit him on fire.

I don't know if I would have, could have done such a thing. I was so frightened, I don't have any idea what I would have done.

Torch in hand, I squirmed and crawled, scratched and kicked my way into the hole. For a second I was wedged tight as a cork, but with a twist of the hips I scraped through.

I kept wriggling forward. The wild man had weapons

and I wanted to get out of reach fast. I kept pushing until the twists and turns led me to a room where I could stand up. Hollering reverberated from the direction I had come but I couldn't make out a word.

I didn't answer. He couldn't touch me here.

I put my life jacket back on. I lit my third torch and I breathed easier. It wasn't possible for the wild man to squeeze through that hole. An anaconda would have an easier time getting through a garden hose.

I was safe, in a manner of speaking. Now I had to find another way out before my last torch failed.

This was insane.

THE FACT THAT I WASN'T FOLLOWING a single footprint
sent a tingle down my spine. I might be the first
human being ever to set foot here, and I might be
exploring my own tomb.

Sometimes I had to get down on my belly and crawl
forward, choking on the oily torch smoke. Sometimes
I had to climb over blocky limestone boulders. Once,
on a steep slope going down, I thought for sure the
passage was pinching shut. But there was another rabbit hole down there. All the time I was mostly moving
to the right and moving down, inside a sort of cork-
screw.

After that I was climbing again, and then it was up
and down and around and around. I lost all sense of
direction. Time was working against me—the head of
the torch was halfway gone. I kept trying to push back
my fear of the light going out, but the fear was gaining
on me. What was I going to do, turn around and try to
wriggle my way blind back to the sea exit? Was that
possible?

As I stood there I heard faint echoes of what
sounded like rushing water. I guessed that a larger cave

was ahead. I followed my torch forward, desperate for a break in my luck.

The passage began to widen. Now it was decorated with fantastic mineral sculptures. The sound of rushing water grew louder and louder. Ahead of me the floor was strewn with bones: ribs, vertebrae, the skulls of small animals with big canine teeth, skulls of bears, and even the skulls and antlers of what had to be caribou.

How old were these bones? How many thousands of years had it been since caribou lived on this island?

Either these animals had died here, or animals or people had dragged them here. There had to be an opening nearby.

I knelt close and peeled my eyes. If only there were human remains, any mark of humans: a scraper, a stone point stuck in one of these bones, picture writing on the walls.

I was so ready to make a big discovery, so ready. But I had no time. There might be something here, but it would take a proper archeological dig to find it. I had to keep going.

I pushed ahead toward the ever-louder sound of rushing water. Seconds later my torchlight fell on a creek flowing through a cavern that took my breath away. It was two hundred feet, easily, from the creek to the monumental stalactites suspended from the ceiling.

Immediately, another surprise: My torch wasn't the only light source. Downstream, the creek and the far slope were lit by natural light from an opening I couldn't quite make out. The only thing was, could I reach it and could I crawl through it?

Motion in the creek caught my eye. There were animals in the water, live animals. Their heads were above the water at times, then suddenly they would disappear.

A couple of harbor seals. They'd swum here from salt water. What did it mean, that the creek emptied into the ocean underwater?

In another minute I found out why the seals were in the cave. One had a salmon in its mouth. Taking a second look at the creek, I recognized the quick flurries of fish running just under the surface.

A salmon run, and seals, and that wasn't all. Suddenly, from behind a formation that looked like a gigantic frosted cupcake, a brown bear rushed into the stream and swatted one of the seals with a crushing blow. The bear turned with the seal in its jaws and climbed the steep slope toward the light.

On the spot, I knew two things. The first was, if a bear could get in, I could get out. The second was, I wasn't going to even think about it until dark, or I might run smack into a bear. In the dark hours they shouldn't be seal hunting.

In the meantime I had about six hours to kill. When my light ran out I had to be within easy reach of the entrance. Right now I had a chance to make a discovery. This place seemed so likely to have been used by ancient people, I could taste it.

I walked upstream alongside flowing white terraces of calcite. No tracks of bears in the muddy places, thank goodness. The rooms were so large it was almost like I was in a canyon outdoors. Everywhere I looked I saw magnificent columns, draperies, icing-covered flowstones, doll houses, castles, tiny rooms tucked in the walls and furnished with exquisite miniatures. Yet, all these works were made by nature. What I wouldn't have given for a single human artifact, or simply some ancient graffiti on the wall.

In between the great rooms the cavern narrowed, but I always found a way to continue on one side of the creek or the other.

I entered a room where the rushing water was much louder than before. It was the most spectacular of all, a grotto, a perfect sphere, with the creek spilling from a tunnel at the far end into a pool that took up most of the grotto's floor. Smooth walking terraces led around the pool on either side. Set back from the terraces were freestanding figures that looked like an army of giants standing guard. The underlying rock that made up their bodies was a rich yellow brown, and it was all topped by layers of bright white calcite icing, giving the giants hoods and capes and teeth and ribs.

The grotto turned out to be as far as I could go. Salmon were leaping up and into the jet of water pouring out of the tunnel at the head of the pool, but I wasn't going to be able to follow. The water in the tunnel would have been chest deep, and there weren't any handholds.

I walked around the side of the great pool, drawn by the place where the creek burst out of the wall.

At the end of the line, I tried to picture ancient people standing exactly where I was standing. This cave would have been quite a wonder; they would have wanted to explore it. Ancient people all over the world had used caves. They were special places, sacred places.

Could they have found a way in?

Yes, through the bears' entrance, or else through the mouth of the creek. Back then, the creek wouldn't have entered the ocean underwater, like it did now. Sea level was three or four hundred feet lower; the stream would have burst out of the cliff, high above the sea, in a spectacular waterfall. The people down below, paddling on the ocean in their skinboats, would have been impressed. Somebody would have said, Let's climb up there and see if we can get inside.

Talk about explorers. They were the originals. Every day, a new world.

I strained to make out pictures on the walls, but they just weren't there. Imagining they had once been, until time and dripping water and minerals had covered them over, made me feel a little less disappointed.

I was about to turn back. My eyes ran up the flowing slope on my side of the stream to a small chamber twenty or so feet above, like an open jewel box decorated with mineral encrustations. Where I was standing was not the last reachable spot in the cave. That little room was.

Torch in hand, I skittered up the slope. In front of the chamber, I perched on a small balcony and looked inside.

I held my breath, afraid to make a sound lest it break the spell. *Here it was*, the prize I'd been hoping to find: a human skull sparkling with a coating of bright gypsum crystals. The chamber was so small, the skull was almost within arm's reach, though it was against the back wall. It took me a few seconds to see that the entire skeleton was there, the bones all covered with gypsum crystals and calcite. Within the crook of the skeleton's arm, on a bed of cave pearls, were three miniature boats carved from ivory.

It was uncanny how close their proportions were to my father's soapstone carving, the one my mother had left at Hidden Falls.

Dad, I thought. Can you see me? I found your proof. A burial, and boats to go with them. Boat people, just as you always figured.

There was even more: in the corner of the chamber, small carvings of seals or sea lions, each with a harpoon sticking out of its body.

My torch was sputtering badly. It was time to go, and quickly. I took another good look, trying to memorize every detail. I removed one boat; it fit in the palm of my hand. The fossilized ivory didn't seem fragile. I tucked it in the deepest pocket of my vest, zipped up my fleece jacket, rebuckled my life jacket. The tiny boat was good and secure.

Time to go. Time to get out of there and get home. I had my prize.

How old was it? That was the question.

While I still had light, I hurried back to within sight

of the entrance the bear had used. Long after my torch had gone out, I waited out the dimming of the natural light from outside. I ate some jerky, dried salmon, and pemmican. When it was all but dark, I made my move.

Knowing full well that a bear might be napping at the opening or very close by, I inched my way through the jagged portal, which reeked with the scent of death. I stumbled across the remains of a small carcass with extremely long finger bones—a harbor seal. It took some time to find my way in the near dark through the maze of trees and boulders outside. I was weary through and through.

What I needed was a safe place to sleep. The stars were coming out, hard and sharp as diamonds. The storm had been replaced by dead calm. The gurgling of a creek down below was the only sound. Through a break in the trees I saw starlight reflected on ocean water. I would stumble over the edge of a cliff if I kept going. I curled into a ball and fell dead asleep.

# 17

I HEARD A FLUTE. I MUST BE DREAMING, I thought, but as I blinked myself awake and shook the cobwebs out of my head, the music was still there.

The sky—what I could see of it from my hiding place—was a hard blue like the sky back home. The sun was dazzling. Animals of some kind were breaking the surface out in the cove. Dolphins? As I shielded my eyes and squinted for a better look I realized they were much larger than that. I was looking at a pod of orca whales. Six or eight black and white orcas were breaching clean out of the water, playing wildly, as if responding to the flute.

If that's what it was, I felt the same way. Something about the beautiful flute melody and this Colorado-blue morning spelled deliverance. Someone had to be playing that flute. Was there a boat in the cove, anchored where I couldn't see it?

Hard experience on this island warned me to play it safe. Careful not to snap a twig or dislodge a rock, I edged closer.

As the head of the cove came into view I could see it was extremely rugged. Cliffs hemmed it in on both sides. The only break in the cliffs was the mouth of the stream I had heard the night before.

As I made my way down the slope, I stopped to watch the whales. Incredibly, they were racing underwater, straight toward the mouth of the creek. I had a good idea that they were rubbing their bellies along the shallow gravels at the head of the cove. I had seen a video of such a thing once, but this was nothing like TV.

A minute later I caught a glimpse of the small gravel beach where the creek entered salt water. Where I had expected to see a boat anchored, there was nothing there. I could still hear the flute.

Suddenly the water erupted at the shore, and the gigantic form of an orca surged onto the beach—after a basking seal or a sea lion? I'd seen orcas do that on the same video. I ran for a better look.

To my amazement, a human form was standing next to the whale, a large figure dressed in bark clothing . . . the wild man.

The flute player and the wild man were one and the same. I watched as he put one hand on the whale's head, just placed it there, and kept playing.

The whale worked its way back into the water and turned itself around. Its tall dorsal fin knifed underwater and the orca was gone.

I backed away. I couldn't begin to understand the wild man, but I knew I had to get away from him. He wasn't any less dangerous because he'd figured out how to call killer whales out of the ocean. The shore was all cliffs; there was nowhere to go but inland. If I kept climbing I would spot a route back to salt water.

A mile up the creek I recognized a downed tree that had fallen across the stream. I'd been here before. This was where I'd crossed with the dog a couple days before. I was only a minute away from the hidden entrance to the trail up to the wild man's alcove. I'd come full circle.

The *tok-tok-tok* of a raven came from the cliffs. It might be the wild man's raven, I thought, and hurried upstream.

The bird took to the air and followed me, croaking from tree to tree. I wished I had a way to shut him up, but silence returned to the forest soon enough. The raven suddenly flew back downstream and disappeared.

I had an idea that soon the wild man would know where I was. After that I suspected every raven I saw.

Bears in the creek ahead, splashing after salmon, forced me steeply up to the right. I climbed the face of the ridge, clawing for handholds in the rock and on the roots of the trees. At the thrashing sound of a raven's wings just above me, I flinched. I looked all around but all I caught was its shadow, and only for a second.

When I finally topped out on the ridge, heaving for breath, what I first took for a bush suddenly stood up. It was the wild man, spear in hand. He said nothing, just looked me up and down.

I was so tired of being afraid of him, I didn't care anymore. If I was under the lion's paw, I wasn't going to act like a rabbit. "It's me," I said. "Nice to see you again. Did you find your dog?"

"No," he said. He was still studying me, looking for answers without asking the questions. I guessed he was wondering how I got out of the cave.

"I'm not surprised," I said. "He's probably running with those wolves. I bet they cover a lot of ground."

The wild man's pale eyes, and then his voice, were full of disdain. "There are no wolves on Admiralty Island."

"Have it your way," I snapped. "But I saw them pretty close. Some were gray, some black. I saw them feeding on a dead orca before I ever ran into you."

"You're making that up. I would know if there were wolves on this island."

I wondered if his voice was rough as sandpaper because he hardly used it, or if his vocal cords were made of sand and gravel and broken bits of seashell. "I know what wolves look like," I insisted.

"Must have been feral dogs you saw."

"Maybe," I allowed, "but I doubt it."

He seemed satisfied that I had backpedaled. Just to be contrary, I said, "Your dog was getting pretty torn up by the alpha male. He's lovesick over one of the females. That's why he took off so fast when he found you weren't home, if you ask—"

The wild man shushed me with a finger to his lips. He had his head cocked to one side, listening.

Then I heard it, the faraway howl of a wolf. No, wolves.

The wild man's rock formation of a face yielded to astonishment. "Wolves," he whispered, his voice etched in wonder. "Wolves on Admiralty."

"Hello . . ." I couldn't help saying.

His stare was as sharp as his spearpoint. "Who are you?"

"Andy Galloway," I said. "I'm from Orchard Mesa, Colorado. Near Grand Junction."

He just kept staring, as if I wasn't making sense.

"You see this life jacket? I was on a sea kayaking trip on Baranof. I got blown over here by a windstorm, lost my kayak."

"And what is it you want?" he asked slowly.

"To get off this island! To get home to my family!"

"Don't shout," he ordered, with a quick glance over his shoulder. "Those *were* wolves. What else do you know about the dog? Do you know a place he might have gone back to?"

Right away I thought of the bear carcass. I remembered how the Newfoundland had fed there, and I remembered the wolf tracks all around. "I do," I said, "but what about you helping me? If I tell you where to find your dog, can you steer me to help? Is that asking too much?"

"I gave you the spear and the knife. It's summer—food everywhere you turn. That should have been enough to get you by."

"Get me by? Your dog is more of a human being than you are."

He bristled like an angry brown bear.

"I'm sick of being scared of you," I told him. "I hate being intimidated. Tell me how to get off this island and I'll tell you where I think you should look for your dog."

His hand went to his chin. The wild man pulled on his beard in an agony of indecision.

"Is there a cabin I can walk to? A place where a fishing boat comes to shore?"

He looked away, bit his lip. "There's a village," he said finally.

"Now we're talking."

"An Indian village, Angoon. The only civilization on the island."

I was so surprised. Here was something valuable. It had nothing to do with wanting to help me. He was this attached to his dog.

"Can you take me there, to the village?"

"No, but I can point the way. There's nothing to it. I have to get my dog before those wolves kill him. That's what they'll do."

"We're going to have to trust each other," I said. "You tell me how to find Angoon, and I'll be straight with you."

He nodded, anxious to get going.

"I saw your dog eating meat from a bear carcass that some poachers killed. Lots of wolf tracks around. I think he'd go back there."

"That's a good bet," the man agreed, "but what's this about poachers?"

"I didn't see them, but they took the hide and the head and feet, and just left the body, all the meat. That has to be against the law. It was disgusting."

He spat on the ground. "Disgustingly legal. But I don't have time to jaw about that. Follow me up here a little ways, I'll set you in the right direction."

We walked a short distance to a bald spot on the ridge where we could see the mountains above. The wild man pointed out two peaks and described a route between them that would lead to the view of an inlet on the other side. I would know it was the right one by its length; it was called Kootznoowoo Inlet, and it poked eight or ten miles into the west side of the island. All I had to do was walk the south shore of that inlet. Angoon was where the inlet met Chatham Strait.

In return I described the landslide scar on the mountain above the carcass, and how the carcass was out on the tundra grass within a stone's throw of the trees. He knew exactly where I was talking about.

We were both eager to go. I couldn't help wondering if he was about to murder me now that he knew what he needed to know. I still didn't know who this wild man was, or what he was about. Suddenly he said, "Leave that bag with me. Take some food out if you want and stuff it inside your life jacket. And when you get close to the village, get rid of those sandals of mine."

I must have looked at him like he was quite a few cards short of a full deck.

"Nobody knows where I live," he explained hoarsely. It wasn't the first time he had told me this. "No need to stir them up," he added.

For the first time I noticed that his teeth were clean and bright as piano keys. So what? I thought, and said, "I hear what you're saying. I understand. Anything I have of yours would give you away."

"I would appreciate it."

He paused uncertainly, then with a grimace, said, "Back at the cannery, I couldn't risk it."

"I understand," I said again, not really understanding at all. All I was thinking was, Just let me walk away, whoever you are, without heaving that spear into my back. You have plenty to hide, and if you let me go, I have plenty to tell.

I took some pemmican and some jerky and stuffed it inside my life jacket. I felt it lodge against the ivory boat in my vest pocket. It didn't look like he was going to going to add any apologies about confining me in his stronghold or chasing me in the cave, which was okay by me. I was never less interested in conversation in my life.

I turned and walked away, and I held my breath. I didn't look back until I was out of spear-chucking range. When I did, the wild man had vanished.

# 18

I STAYED ALONG THE BACKBONE of the ridge. All the while I kept my sights on the two peaks I had to pass between. Luckily they were staying visible. So many days, there wouldn't have been a chance. My ridge was going to lead me all the way to timberline. I shouldn't run into any bears; they were down on the creeks gorging on salmon.

I was crossing Admiralty without a weapon of any kind. I'd accidentally left the stone-bladed knife behind when I fled the alcove. The wild man had probably discovered it, and he hadn't given it back to me. I had to wonder if he was telling the truth about Angoon. Maybe Angoon was fifty miles to the north and as unreachable as Mars. Maybe the wild man was counting on the island to kill me.

I couldn't tell. What I remembered most vividly was his saying that nobody had ever found his hideaway before. It was how he said it, his face, his eyes, his voice. He seemed to be telling me that he was at my mercy.

If he was telling the truth about Angoon, and I was shortly going to find my way out of this mess, he had taken a huge risk. He'd trusted me.

This was something to think about, and I thought about it a lot on my way to timberline. My spirits were soaring as high as the eagles. If I crested the north-south divide of the island between those two peaks and found a deep inlet at my feet that arrowed out to Chatham Strait, I was homeward bound. I had no doubt I could split those peaks before the day was out. The island wasn't that wide. Sometime the next day, I would walk into that village.

No doubt Angoon was hooked up to the rest of the world by phone, fax, and e-mail. I was already rehearsing what I would say when I got hold of my mother. She was going to lose it, just lose it. A second after she got off the phone she would run down the lane to my grandparents' house, and then they would go crazy. They'd all start yelling so loud we might lose the entire peach crop. This close to ripe, all that fruit would just fall to the ground.

The next call I'd make would be to Adventure Alaska, to get a message to Monica and Julia. Then I'd call Derek. As casually as I could manage, I'd say, "Whazzup?"

With Darcy, I'd just ask how she did at the horse show, maybe ask if she's been out at the lake. She'd sound real serious and a little bit spooky. "Is this a joke?" And I'd say, "Why'd you say that?" and she'd say, "It really is you! You're supposed to be dead." And I'd say something like, "Somebody forgot to tell me."

Who knew what I was going to say, or what they'd

say, but it sure was fun thinking about it.

I came out of the trees at practically a gallop and shot straight as an arrow across the tundra toward the slot between those peaks. The deer were plentiful up there. They were built stocky, quite a bit smaller than the mule deer back home. Switching their black tails, they just stood and stared at me. I could picture the wild man stalking them with his bow and arrow or his atlatl. The deer would think they were looking at a bush or something and . . . *thwack* . . . lights out.

Was he a fugitive or wasn't he?

Whatever he was, he was beyond strange.

Suddenly I heard a *whump-whump-whump, chop-chop-chop*. I looked over my shoulder and saw a helicopter coming over the peaks. It seemed to be heading my way. They're coming for me, was my first thought, but of course they weren't. The chopper began to bank to the south.

Fast as I could I unbuckled my life jacket and started to wave it like a crazy man. I jumped up and down, yelling and hollering and waving for dear life.

There was only a small chance that someone was looking my way out of the side window. I was sure the chopper was gone for good when it turned on a dime, swung back around, and headed straight for me.

I couldn't believe my luck, just flat out couldn't believe I wasn't dreaming. Nothing on this island came so easy.

Lo and behold, there they were above me, checking me out, the pilot and a woman next to him. She was pointing down at me, or pointing out a place to land, I couldn't tell which.

Land they did, about a hundred yards away, in a loud and windy fury. I'd never seen anything so beautiful in my life as that metal-and-glass dragonfly and the woman who climbed out of it.

I grabbed my life jacket and ran toward her. She was crouching as she ran under the whipping copter blades. We almost collided. I was like a drowning man reaching for a life buoy. She had beautiful rich brown skin and long, straight hair as black as coal—an Alaskan Indian, I guessed. Her cap said U.S. FISH AND WILDLIFE SERVICE, and the nameplate on her starched gray uniform read SHAYLA MATLOCK. She was ten years younger, maybe, than my mother. Over the roar of the helicopter she leaned toward me and yelled, "What's going on?"

"I could use a ride," I yelled back.

The look on her face said I looked bad, real bad. "Are you by yourself, or what?" she shouted.

"My name's Andy Galloway. I—"

"Holy smoke, I know who you are. Are you starved?"

"I'm okay," I told her.

"I'm happy to hear it. C'mon, let's go."

As I climbed aboard, the man at the controls was checking me out. I must have looked like a dirtball. I could have cared; I was safe.

"It's that Galloway kid who supposedly drowned over on Baranof," Shayla told the pilot, whose nameplate said RIVERS. She buckled me into one of the back seats, and herself into the one alongside. "Am I right?" she asked. "Are you that one?"

"That's me," I was happy to say. Shayla handed me a candy bar and a bottle of water.

"You okay?" the pilot asked, and I said, "Never better."

"We've got a job to do near here, and then we'll get you taken care of. Tell me quick—how'd you end up on Admiralty? Whale spit you out?"

"Wind," I said. He just nodded, and then, after stroking his mustache, he was all business. He put his headphones on, revved up the motor, and we lifted off.

I couldn't believe it. I was airborne. I was out of there.

Shayla Matlock turned to loading a small rifle with something that wasn't a bullet. "Tranquilizer dart," she explained. My eyes fell on a large kennel cage and a hand-held antenna connected to a small black box, but I didn't think anything of any of it. I was just so happy to be rescued.

We'd no more gotten started, it seemed, than we were landing. Rivers put the helicopter down close to the trees in a high mountain meadow. The deer scattered. "What's going on?" I asked.

"We're wildlife biologists," Shayla answered. "Admiralty is part of our territory. We're going to try to take out a dog that's been running with some wolves. We're afraid it will breed with them. We have to get it off the island."

I was still in a daze. It took me a second to register

that she was talking about the Newfoundland, and then it hit me between the eyes. If I opened my mouth I was going to give away the wild man. A few hours before, he had thrown himself at my mercy.

I said nothing at all, just gave a hand unloading the kennel cage. What about the sandals I was wearing? Maybe they wouldn't notice.

Shayla and I watched as Rivers disappeared into the trees with a pack on his back and the tranquilizer gun in his hand. He had a can of pepper spray holstered at his hip; Shayla was wearing one too. "There's a carcass about a mile from here," she told me. "We're hoping the dog we're after will still be there. I was on foot yesterday when I spotted them. Gary's going to go ahead; I'll follow after fifteen minutes with the kennel cage."

"What are you going to do with the dog after you catch him?"

"Take him to the Humane Society in Juneau. I hope he's not vicious, so he'll have a chance of being adopted."

My mind was going this way and that. I didn't know whether to side with these wildlife people or the wild man. He was going to take this hard, real hard. "How long have the wolves been on the island?" I asked.

"Only a month or so, we think. They started up at the northern end."

"Is it a big deal, wolves on the island?"

"It's a very big deal. They haven't been on Admiralty for as long as anybody can tell. My people—we're Tlingits—have been at Angoon for a couple of thousand years at least, and this is a new one for us. It's exciting, because the wolves are going to change the ecological balance, and probably for the better. The deer are too thick for their own good. They would be stronger and healthier if they had the wolf as a predator."

"What about the bears? Don't they snag the deer?"

"Not that often. They get a few fawns the first couple days after they're born. After that, even the fawns are too fast. Plus, the deer tend to stay up high all summer, in the open where the grass is. They can see the bears a long way off. They don't come down into the forest much until the snow forces them down, and that's when the bears are going into hibernation. The bears mostly get the old deer and the sick ones."

"So the wolves should do real well on the Fortress of the Bears."

"Definitely. Say, do you know why Admiralty is called that?"

I shrugged. "Because the bears rule?"

She laughed. "Fortress of the Bears is the Tlingit name for the island. Kootznoowoo. But you're right. Bears rule, that's what it means."

"So the Fish and Wildlife Service reintroduced the wolves?"

She shook her head emphatically. "No, we had nothing to do with it. We figure that they swam from the mainland about a mile and half to Grand Island, and then another mile and a half to Admiralty on the Glass Peninsula. That's where they were first spotted. From the very beginning we worried about dogs from

Angoon. Dogs can go feral and live off the land. It would be a shame for a small wolfpack like this to interbreed with domestic dogs, and it could happen. They'd be hybrids after that, not wolves."

"Is the dog you're after from Angoon?"

"Nobody from the village has ever had a dog like that. It appears to be a purebred Newfoundland. We're not really sure, but we think it belongs to a legend."

"What do you mean, legend?"

"A big black dog was seen a few years ago with a man people say lives in the woods. It was a very brief sighting. There's a lot of debate about whether the man really exists."

"Who's he supposed to be?"

"A hermit. People call him the hermit of Admiralty Island."

I T WAS TIME FOR SHAYLA to follow with the kennel cage. She started to say I should wait by the helicopter, but I was much too involved. I offered to carry the kennel cage, and she agreed. "When the time comes, and I ask you to keep a low profile, how low can you keep it?"

"Pond scum," I assured her.

The biologist shouldered her backpack. "Okay then, let's get going. We'll walk just inside the trees. Keep your eye out for a strip of orange survey tape. Gary's going to flag the spot where we should watch and wait."

I was dying to find out what she knew about the wild man. I caught up and walked alongside. Keeping my voice low, I asked, "So, about that hermit? Do you think it's just a legend, or is he for real?"

"That's a fascinating question," she replied. "Over the past eight or ten years, there have been only a handful of sightings. A couple of them were highly credible, and one was by the man I replaced in this job. He's the one, a few years back, who saw the big black dog with him."

"He got a good look?"

"Good, but brief. They disappeared in the trees."

"And you spotted a Newfoundland running with the wolves you've been watching?"

"About ten days ago. Actually, we darted him back then."

I was so surprised, I lost focus and stumbled over a tree root. "Once you'd caught him, why didn't you take him off the island?"

"We were trying to kill two birds with one stone. You see, we turned him loose after sewing up a radio transmitter inside his body, just under his last rib."

"You're kidding. What for?"

"We were hoping he would lead us to the hermit's hideaway. We assume he must have one. But since we released him, the dog has never stayed in one place for more than a few hours. Gary and I have been tramping all over the southern end of the island, keeping tabs on him, mostly from up high where the walking is easier. We would have tracked him from an airplane or the helicopter, but we were afraid of tipping off the hermit. It could be his hiding place is on this end of the island."

"Is the wild man a fugitive or something? Is he dangerous? Is that why you want to find him?"

"As far as anyone knows, he's perfectly harmless. As to whether he's a fugitive, that's another question. There are several theories."

"Wait a second. I don't get it. If you catch the dog today, you're going to fly it to Juneau, right?"

"Right. And while we're at it, we can drop you off at the airport. You'll be on a jet home in no time."

"Sounds great, but how does that help you catch the wild man—the hermit?"

"It doesn't. We've decided to give up on that for now. It's more important that we prevent the dog and the wolves from mating."

"Okay, okay, I got that. . . . Now, tell me about those theories. One is, he's a fugitive?"

"That's one school of thought, and the most popular. Some people think he must be an escaped convict, and others think he's a guy who owes jail time in the Lower Forty-eight but never served it. A tax evader or who-knows-what. Alaska's always been known for that sort of thing—good place to adopt a new identity, start over, more or less hide out. This would be an extreme case, of course."

"What are the other possibilities?"

"That he's an extreme survivalist. Hates the government, is waiting for the end of the world, that sort of thing."

"You don't sound like you go for any of those theories."

"I don't. A few of us science types have our own take on this. We have a theory that he was an archeologist."

As soon as she said the word "archeologist," my mind went this way and that. Struggling to keep my voice level, I asked, "How does that one go?"

"It's just a wild guess. Ten or eleven years ago, there was an archeologist who drowned off the shore of Chichagof Island, across the Chatham Strait from Admiralty. He was by himself. Apparently he fell out of a boat that he rented to go fishing. That type of accident happens every so often up here. Only half the time do they find the body. They never found his."

An *archeologist*, I thought. It had been so close I couldn't see it. Just because you're an archeologist doesn't mean you have to teach at a university, like my father did, and just because you're an archeologist doesn't mean you can't be crazy. "I don't follow," I told her after what had been a lengthy pause. "Why can't a guy who falls out of a boat haul himself back in?"

"I didn't explain that the boat is moving. The fisherman is trolling—let's say for salmon. He stands up, loses his balance, goes over the side. Now he's in the freezing Pacific, watching his boat get farther and farther away. It's that simple."

"So in the cold water, he's history. But what makes you think the hermit is that archeologist?"

"The first time he was ever sighted, he had a spear in his hand, that's all. Someone in our office thought to link him with the archeologist. Some archeologists know how to make stone points, that sort of thing. It's just speculation, but it's intriguing to think about."

"If he survived the accident, why didn't he come for help? Why would he hide out, become a hermit?"

"That's the part where you really have to make a few leaps. It's all pretty far-fetched."

The bulky kennel cage was beginning to feel like a ton of bricks, even though it wasn't that heavy. Rather than stop for a rest, and risk this conversation getting sidetracked, I switched hands and said the next thing that popped into my head. "Wait a second. You think he faked his own death? Is that it?"

"It could be done," she replied. "Let's say somebody wanted to do that. When they find your boat with your fishing line in the water and the motor in gear, it's going to look like one of your typical southeast Alaska boating accidents. What a perfect way to disappear, if that's what you're trying to do."

"But why would he want to disappear? Who was the archeologist? Does anybody know?"

"His name has slipped my mind. It was so long ago the newspapers reported it. They said he was from the Lower Forty-eight. A college professor."

"You figure he wanted to leave it all behind, to become a hermit?"

She looked over her shoulder at me and she chuckled. "You're pretty into this."

"It's amazing to think about. I just can't figure out why anyone would want to be a hermit. That's crazy. Especially on an island like this."

"Your guess is as good as mine. I do know that some people live and die by convictions so strong that most people can't even comprehend them. Maybe the hermit of Admiralty Island is one of those."

All of this had me reeling, trying to reinterpret everything that had happened between me and the wild man. Maybe what had been going on was very different from what I *thought* was going on. He could have been just as weirded out as I was. I might have been the first person he talked to in ten or eleven years.

Shayla called a rest break. We were both winded

from talking while we were climbing. The biologist's eyes happened to go to my feet, to the wild man's cedar bark sandals. For the first time, she really noticed them. Her dark eyes were awash in speculation. I thought that if I kept talking, she might not ask. "I still don't get it," I said. "Why were you trying to catch him? Was he doing something wrong?"

Shayla was slow to answer. "You just asked a very tough question, Andy. If we ever do catch him, it's going to be a real shame. It will be very hard to explain to the people in Angoon, for example. They'll think it's senseless. The short answer is, Admiralty Island National Monument has a new superintendent. It really bothers him that, for all these years, someone has been hunting, fishing, camping on the island without permits or permission. . . ."

"So?"

"I know. That doesn't sound like a big deal. Admiralty is public land, which means it belongs to all of us, but there have to be rules and regulations."

I immediately thought of my father. I could picture him, with all his prehistoric skills, maybe wanting to try it for himself in some wilderness somewhere. Maybe he would have, for a while at least, if he hadn't had a family.

"Still, that's lame," I said. "They should make an exception if you're willing to live in the Stone Age."

She shrugged, and we tramped on. A few minutes later Shayla was pointing. "Look," she whispered. "Up ahead. Gary's survey tape."

Shayla eased her backpack to the ground and

removed a huge pair of binoculars. "Leave the kennel cage here for now. Let's belly up to the edge of the trees and see what we can see."

Through the branches, as we crept close, I made out the huge mound of red flesh on the tundra. I squinted at a blur of motion nearby. I saw the black dog and the gray wolf.

So did Shayla. "We're in business," the biologist said. "This is good. From their behavior, I'd say they haven't mated yet. Here, take a look."

I couldn't believe the magnification. I could see the gray wolf's black lips against the white hairs on her muzzle and lower jaw. Her ears were white inside and rimmed with darker fur, and her yellow eyes were set off by black eyelids. I could see the dark tip of her tail. The wolf and the Newfie were licking each other's faces, and now they were rubbing cheeks, and now they were mouthing each other's muzzles. "Isn't she magnificent?" Shayla whispered at my shoulder.

"Totally," I whispered back, thinking they both were. "Where's your partner?"

"Hidden. Waiting for the right moment. He'll want the dog a little closer."

I could only wonder where the wild man was. I had sent him here. He could have walked right into the middle of this.

No, he was much too cautious for that.

If only he'd gotten here in time. . . .

What was I thinking? Whose side was I on?

I really didn't know.

Shayla nudged my elbow. "Tell me what you're seeing."

"I see the dog tearing off a piece of meat. . . . She's kind of moving away. . . . She's looking at him sideways, looking back at the trees. Now she's edging closer to the trees. This is getting good. . . . He's coming over to her with the meat, kind of holding it up high."

"Courtship behavior."

"He's putting his mouth next to hers."

"Offering food."

"But she kind of jumps away. She won't take it."

"She's suspicious. It's got human scent all over it. It's tainted. She knows better."

The Newfoundland ate the meat as the wolf, tail down, retreated closer to the trees. "I think she's about to take off," I whispered. "Here, you look."

"No, you. You might never see something like this again."

I thanked her, and had just shifted my view back to the dog when a gun suddenly went off. It wasn't a rifle blast, it was more of a pop, like from an air gun. I spotted the tranquilizer dart right away. "Did Gary hit him?" Shayla asked urgently.

"Right in the shoulder," I reported. I tried for a glimpse of the wolf's reaction, but she had vanished. I still couldn't see the location of the shooter. Rivers was staying hidden.

I passed the binoculars to Shayla. Even without them, I could see the dog staggering. Then he dropped.

# 20

"GRAB THE KENNEL CAGE, ANDY."

By the time we got there, Rivers was out on the tundra, sitting cross-legged and making notes on a laptop computer. I checked out my old friend, the Newfoundland. He was out cold. The blue material I'd wrapped around his neck was long gone. The wound on his ear had healed and the one on his neck looked much better. I felt pretty bad about him going to the pound.

After a minute I tore myself away and walked toward the carcass. The ravens were busy. They were keeping an eye on me, but they didn't think I was much of a threat. Shayla was at my shoulder. She seemed about to ask me something. I had a feeling it would be about my sandals and whether I knew more than I was saying about the hermit. "So this is legal?" I asked instead. "Killing bears on the Fortress of the Bears?"

She bit her lip. "That's a sore spot with me. Just between you and me, I can't believe it's still going on."

"I mean, the bear's all mutilated."

"That's how they do it, to get what they need for their bearskin rugs. The fur, the claws—it's trophy hunting, pure and simple, but it's legal. Sometimes all they're after is getting a photograph of themselves next to the dead bear."

"They should have to take out all the meat, and then they should have to eat it."

"That would discourage them, all right. Not many people consider brown bear fit to eat. That's why Alaska Fish and Game doesn't require them to take out the meat. Most years they allow around ninety bear kills on Admiralty. The skull is missing because the hunters are required to turn them in, partly so the game wardens can keep track, and partly so they can study them. From the teeth they can tell the age of the bear."

"I'm confused. You aren't a game warden?"

"They work for the state. Even though it's federal land, the state takes care of hunting and fishing licenses and so on."

"Let's load him up," called Rivers as he was stowing his laptop computer away in his backpack.

"Will do," his partner replied cheerfully. "I'm sure Andy is anxious to get started home."

"Am I ever," I agreed.

Just then, at the edge of my vision, there was motion. The biologists had seen something too. We all turned our heads, and there was the man in bark. With his eyes on us, he'd been inching toward the dog. Now that he was exposed, halfway between the forest and his dog, he hesitated like a runner caught between bases.

Rivers bolted toward the Newfoundland but the wild man was even faster. With several huge bounding strides, he cut off the biologist's approach, then stood up to his full height, which was considerable. The wild man held his massive arms and hands up high, raking the air like a bear, and then he *roared*, horribly and convincingly, like a brown bear. His scarred features left little doubt that he meant to defend his dog.

Rivers's right hand went to the pepper spray at his hip, but instead of pulling it out, he shrank toward his partner. When he did, the wild man spun back to his dog. He went to one knee, removed the tranquilizer dart, scooped up that big Newfoundland in his arms, and stood. For a moment he paused, and his eyes found mine. He looked hurt, he looked bewildered.

Suddenly, without a backward glance, the wild man ran into the forest, the huge dog in his arms.

I turned to Shayla. She was dumbfounded, and so was Rivers.

"Well," Shayla said at last, "I believe we just met the hermit of Admiralty Island."

"Up close and personal," her partner added. He was still shaking his head.

I didn't say a word. As we made our way back to the helicopter, the biologists were so preoccupied they didn't seem to notice I was there. Rivers was saying that this was going to turn out for the best. The hermit was going to keep his dog real close, maybe even tie him for a while, and that would make it easy to track him and find his hideaway.

Shayla agreed. The thing is, neither one of them sounded victorious. They sounded sad.

All the way back to the helicopter, I was turning it

over in my mind, all of it. One helicopter ride and I'd be at a telephone talking to my mother. It would all be over.

Time seemed to accelerate. I was about to board the helicopter.

This just wasn't right.

At the last second, I couldn't get in the helicopter. "Just a minute," I said. "I gotta use the trees."

Shayla chuckled and said, "Go ahead. Gary has a few last-minute checks, anyway."

I made for the trees and kept on going. After a while I heard them calling, but I was already long gone.

I had to get back to the wild man, had to warn him. Time was everything. I had to pick the right route, but the terrain looked so different from this direction. Twice I lost my way. The second time it meant climbing clear out of the wrong creek valley. I heard the helicopter above the forest a couple of times, but there was no chance they could see me. I hurried. I just hoped I could reach the wild man in time.

As I got close, the daylight was fading. A raven was following from tree to tree. It could have been any raven, but I had a feeling it was his. I heard the droning sound of an airplane motor in the direction of the coast. The airplane wasn't very far away but oddly, I couldn't hear it anymore. It had probably landed in the cove. I figured out what must be going on. Shayla and Rivers had tracked the wild man from the helicopter. When he stopped moving, they knew he'd arrived at his camp. Within a little area they knew right where to look. But there was no place to land the helicopter because of the forest. They'd called in a floatplane.

It was a footrace now. As I started up the zigzag path to the alcove I listened for searchers, but I couldn't hear a thing. The raven flew croaking toward the overhang. From high on the cliff I saw motion downstream and then the glint of a hand-held antenna.

As I reached the end of the high ledge I was greeted by the Newfoundland on the other side. He wagged his tail at me, waved his head. I strained to see beyond him.

The wild man appeared out of the shadows, trembling. His features were distorted with volcanic anger. "How dare you come back here?"

After my climb, I was still bent over double and gasping for breath. "Quick," I managed, keeping my voice down. "Lower that thing and let me—"

"Have they sent you to—"

"I'm not with them!" I pleaded. "Not so loud! They're down there, they're coming!"

"How can you say you're not with them when I saw you with them? What do they want?"

I'd had enough. "Listen to me, fool! They spotted me, they picked me up. I didn't breathe a word about you. I ran all this way to *warn* you. Feel under your dog's last rib—I don't know which side. They sewed a radio transmitter inside him about ten days ago. There's guys right down there with an antenna, do you get it?"

He was overwhelmed, totally confused. He tried the dog's right side, then the left side. He gave me a strange look. "There *is* something here."

"Take it out and smash it. Hurry, before they figure out how close they are!"

The wild man lowered the bridge and I hurried across. He ran and grabbed a knife.

At the edge of the alcove, where the light was best, I sat cross-legged with the dog's head on my foreleg and stroked the crown of his head.

"The knife is so sharp you'll never notice," the wild man said to his dog, who rolled his eyes from the knife to the man and seemed reassured. He laid his head back down on my leg.

The wild man parted the thick fur and exposed the incision the biologists had made. The stitches had mostly fallen out; the wound had already healed.

A single yelp from the dog, and the wild man held up the transmitter between his thumb and forefinger. It was plastic, shaped like an egg. He raised it high, then smashed it against the bedrock. Now it was nothing but shards of plastic and metal and silicon chips.

I peered over the edge of the alcove. He joined me. There were two men in forest-service green down there with packs on their backs and rifles over their shoulders. They stopped and switched on their flashlights. I asked if the dog would bark.

"Not at a time like this," the wild man whispered. "What were they going to do with the dog?"

"He was headed for the Humane Society in Juneau, so he couldn't mate with the wolves. They darted him once before. That's when they planted the transmitter, to get to you."

He was still looking at me strangely, like I'd dropped in from the moon and brought all this down on his head. "But why would they be trying to track me? What conceivable reason?"

I told him about the new superintendent of Admiralty National Monument. Shaking his head, he said, "Dumbest thing I ever heard. But I believe it."

"Can you stitch your dog?"

"No need, he's barely bleeding. He's okay."

The men down below were fooling with a small black box like the one I'd seen in the helicopter. "What are they doing?" the wild man fretted.

"They're trying to figure out why the signal went dead—if the problem is on their end or with the transmitter."

"Do you think they know how close they are?"

"I hope not."

"This could be the end," the wild man said, tearing at his beard. Keeping low, he crept back into the alcove. With a glance over my shoulder, I saw him hurriedly collecting some of his tools and stowing them in one of his hide bags. "Pull the bridge up," he said, "as quietly as you can. Then keep an eye on them and tell me if they find the way up."

I did as he told me. When I got back down on my belly and looked over the edge, I was shocked to see the flashlight beams stabbing this way and that, close to the big downed tree that hid the foot of the trail.

I scuttled over to warn him. He was selecting fishhooks and what appeared to be bone needles, placing them in a small wooden box. "They're close to finding the foot of the trail."

"Go back. Tell me if they find it."

I scuttled back and looked over the edge. No doubt about it, they had found the spot behind the downed spruce where the trail began. The question was, would they climb those rock ledges to investigate? Or would they wait until morning?

The answer wasn't long in coming. They were on the first pitch. The beams were flashing this way and that. They were looking for the way up.

"They're coming up," I reported breathlessly. "They just set their rifles aside."

The wild man grabbed his bow drill and began to work it immediately, with an amazing economy of motion. His dog stood close, watching intently. In no time at all the spindle was making sawdust. In less than a minute the wild man had a live coal. Touching old man's beard to his coal, he had flame. "I have one torch left," he whispered. "Tucked behind that box."

Then I knew. "You're going to use your boat," I said as I handed him the torch. "Your skinboat."

"Yes," he said. "It's time to leave this island. But the dog is terrified of the cave. Won't go in it. I don't know if this will work. I can't hold the torch and carry him at the same time."

Maybe I should have thought it through, but there just wasn't time. I could feel it in my gut, which side I was on. "I'll hold the torch," I told him.

He was incredulous. "You? This is your chance—they have an airplane."

"Can you take me somewhere, somewhere I can get home?"

The wild man hesitated, then nodded. He lit his torch and placed it in my hand. For a second it looked like he was going to say thank you. He placed the bow drill in his carrying bag and slung it over his shoulder. The bag looked heavy; he must have thrown in a bunch of his stone tools. Even so, he reached down and lifted the dog.

From nearby came a familiar croak. "What about that raven?" I asked.

"He's been with me his whole life, but the world is his playground. Let's go."

I led toward the cave opening at the far end of the alcove. The torchlight fell on the wild man's amazing mural of prehistoric America. I stopped for a glance back, and found him taking a last look at his cliff home and the hundreds upon hundreds of artifacts he was leaving behind. How much time, I wondered, to make even a single axhead?

The searchers must have been nearing the top of the trail. One of their beams bounced off the ceiling. Some of the reflected light struck the mural and then the wild man's tortured features.

We started inside.

21

THE DOG WHINED AND CRIED and yelped something awful. Before we were even out of the twilight zone and into the dark, he was thrashing so violently that the wild man couldn't continue. He set the Newfoundland down among the bear skulls and tried to calm him. At the muffled sound of voices calling—the two men must have been shouting from the ledge across from the alcove—the dog perked up his ears. "Let's get going," the wild man said as he lifted the big Newfoundland again and carried him, whimpering, into the absolute darkness.

As soon as torchlight was all there was, the wild man set his dog down on a smooth run of calcite. The poor dog was trembling, spooked by the sound of dripping water, by every echo. He ran into the darkness this way and that. Each time, he came back trembling and whining to the torch. After that he was so close on the wild man's heels it was difficult for the big man to walk. I was nearly as spooked. All I could think about was how I could have been headed home. Crazy, to take another risk, and for the wild man. What was he to me?

I had a bad feeling about this.

We passed into the caverns with fantastic decorations, threaded our way around the blue pools, and entered the atrium room with the ceiling almost too high to see. We put the six emerald pools behind us, the maze too. The big dog was no longer making a sound but was sticking closer than ever to the wild man, eyes going this way and that, as if doom might strike at any second. I was afraid he had a sixth sense, and even more than that, I was remembering how I fell into an abyss in the cave dream I had when I was paralyzed.

My dread grew worse as we approached the pit, the immense circular well—the abyss. I felt disconnected from my body, dizzy, weak all over.

"Careful," called the wild man from behind.

"I know," I managed to reply as I started across the ledge. I knew better, but I couldn't keep my eyes off the void below me. Suddenly the ledge was no wider than a balance beam, like in the dream, or so it felt. My knees were shaking; I was shaking all over.

Maybe the Newfoundland suddenly became aware of the danger. Maybe the wild man should have been carrying him across. I heard something going wrong, looked over my shoulder. Somehow the dog had gotten tangled in the man's feet, and the man, trying to stay upright, lurched into the dog.

The dog yelped, and a cry escaped the wild man's throat. I saw first his shadow and then his huge form where it never should have been, off balance and slipping off the ledge. There was nothing I could do; the wild man was falling.

I was expecting the worst—a thud or a splash from far below. For some bizarre reason there was no sound other than the whimpering of his dog. I was sure the hermit was gone for good, but I willed myself to peer over the edge. I held the torch out carefully, and there was his face, eight or ten feet below. He was well out of reach, clinging by his fingers to a lip of calcite. From his waist up, he was on a sickeningly steep slope. I couldn't see below his hips. He was halfway over a sheer drop-off.

I knew he wouldn't be able to hold on long. His body weight and the stone tools in the bag on his back were pulling him down.

The torchlight caught his pale eyes. It was taking the tenacity of all his years in the wilderness to hang on. His dog saw him too, and was whimpering worse than before.

*Do something*, my mind screamed, but there wasn't a thing I could do. I didn't have a rope. How was it possible he was still hanging on?

The wild man was even stronger than I had imagined. With the time his supreme effort bought him, he must have been able to place one of his feet. His head and shoulders moved upward some. A free hand reached for a new grip but couldn't find one. It was all smooth rock.

I had an idea. I set the torch aside, pulled off my long fleece pants. Now that he was a little closer they might reach. If I held on to one pant leg, he might be able to grab hold of the other.

I planted myself as best I could, gritted my teeth. He

made his move. With his right hand, he snatched his end. The force was tremendous. It threatened to pull me down. In the heat of the moment my full strength was back, and then some. I heard the trousers rip and I was afraid the pants were about to come apart.

Somehow they held together, and the wild man gained enough leverage to lift a foot above the lip. However he did it he was climbing, reaching for a grip with his free left hand.

I kept pulling. He was coming on up.

I gave a last heave. The wild man was up and over. He lay sprawled on the ledge, all out of breath. Both of us and the dog moved as far from the edge as possible. I pulled my torn pants back on, over my thermal underwear.

Still gulping air, the wild man said gravely, "I thank you." He reached out for the Newfoundland, who was shaking all over.

"Forget it," I told him.

"I never hollered for help," he said.

I couldn't believe what I'd just heard. I said, "You came within a gnat's eyelash of going down. Or was I missing something?"

"It's just that I came to this island to live and die—if it came to that—without help. By my own rules."

"You should have put up a sign."

"Don't get me wrong," he said with deep feeling. "I'm very happy to be alive. You say 'Forget it,' but I don't believe I ever will. You amaze me no end. Coming back to warn me like you did, then saving my life—

there's no accounting for it. I'm baffled. You're a complete mystery to me."

I couldn't help laughing. It burned off some of the fear. I was still in shock. "You're kidding. It's the other way around."

We got up and continued on through the cave until a breeze fluttered the torch. It was coming from the rabbit hole.

"Clear this much up for me," the wild man said. "Yesterday, how come you went through that little hole there? Didn't you hear me yelling that you were going to get yourself killed?"

"I couldn't make out the words. Anyway, I was scared out of my mind. How about if you tell me: Why did you trap me at your camp when you ran off to find your dog?"

"I thought when I got back I would try to explain my situation to you, figure out what to do. Then I came back and found you'd started a fire and gone into the cave. I figured you must be crazy. I didn't know what to think."

"I know what I thought. I thought you were a big-time bogeyman. I was taking my chances there was another way out of the cave."

"Is there?"

"There is."

"I assumed you must have hidden in the cave till I left, then come back through my camp while I was away."

I could barely believe it. This was a whole lot like a

normal conversation. He was starting to act almost human, like he'd suddenly remembered what words were for.

Keep it going, I thought. I said, "It's hard to tell the difference on this island between what you think is happening and what is really happening."

"True," he said solemnly. "So true. The line goes back and forth. It's a place out of time, the Fortress of the Bears. The reality you bring with you fades quickly. Dream country, that's what it is. Some things you can find an explanation for. Others you never will. But I'm still curious about this hole you disappeared into, and what you saw when you squeezed through it. I could never fit."

"You could have bashed it bigger with your stone tools and explored it yourself."

He shrugged. "I haven't wanted to leave my mark on this island."

"Your mural," I couldn't help pointing out. "What about your amazing mural?"

"I meant to erase it—chip it back to bedrock—before I ever left."

"That would have been a crime. I'm glad you never got the chance."

"I was once an archeologist, you see."

"That's just what she guessed—Shayla, the wildlife biologist."

"Did she, now?"

"She said that most people thought you must be a fugitive."

"They were wrong, she was right."

"She didn't know your name."

He realized I was asking for it. "It's David," he said hesitantly. "David Atkins."

From someone hiding from the world, this was a mouthful. "I have to ask you about your mural," I began. "About the Clovis hunters coming across the land bridge. Did you—"

"Clovis? You know about Clovis?"

"Your spearpoint is a Clovis replica. I saw that the second I laid eyes on it."

"You keep surprising me."

On impulse I said, "You ain't seen nothing yet, wild man." I unbuckled my life jacket and brought out the ivory boat. The small carving gleamed in the torchlight like a magic talisman.

"Well, would you look at that," he whispered. "Incredible." The former archeologist was awestruck. He took the carving in his hands and examined it closely. His dog sniffed it with great interest.

"What do you make of it?" I asked eagerly.

"It's an effigy of a skinboat, I'm almost positive. You found this in the cave?"

"And more," I couldn't help saying. "Is it walrus ivory?"

"Mammoth ivory."

From Asia, I thought, not from North America.

"If it was walrus," he added, "it would have an amber tint. Mammoth ivory is white. It's pretty similar to elephant ivory." He put the boat back in my hands. "We better hurry," he said. "Time and tide wait for no man. Promise you'll tell me more when we get on the water."

One last twist in the meanderings of the cave, and we could see faint light reflected off the surface of the last pool.

We launched his skinboat. David Atkins stepped into the stern, I stepped into the bow, the big dog jumped in between us. The Newfoundland was eager. He could smell the open air.

The tide was lower than when I'd attempted this before. As we cleared the opening we found the stars out, and there was quite a bit of light from a half moon. It was all so calm and peaceful, nothing like I'd found it before. We paddled out of the tight V formed by the cliffs and into the wider bay. I was so relieved to be on the water and to be putting Admiralty behind me at last. "Now, how do I get home? Where can you take me?"

"Kake. It's a Tlingit Indian village across the water on the next island, Kupreanof. From there you can fly to Juneau or Petersburg."

"This skinboat—can it make the crossing?"

"Of course. I've done it before."

"If you say so, David. What kind of skins are these?"

"Seal."

"Your Newfoundland—does he have a name?"

"Bear. His name is Bear."

"I should have guessed. Suits him, suits the island. Those wildlife biologists don't think he came from Angoon. So, where did he come from?"

"I can only guess. I found him wandering around

lost. Off some boat probably, fishing boat or sailboat."

"Before him, did you have another dog?"

"I had a bear once, an orphan cub. For a while I had them both, but I had to kick the bear out after two winters, like his mother would have."

Suddenly I remembered my strange encounter with the bear that had sat beside me. I told Atkins all about it and he busted out with a deep belly laugh. It was the first time I'd heard him laugh; I wouldn't have thought he was capable of it. "Oh, that's him, no doubt about it. There isn't another bear on Admiralty that would've behaved like that around a dog or a human. I'm surprised the bear hunters haven't gotten him by now."

"Did your bear give you that mark on your face?"

"Yeah, sometimes he played rough."

"What about your bearskin sleeping bag? Did you kill that bear?"

"I scavenged that skin."

"Have you ever had to defend yourself with your spear?"

"Came close a couple of times. There's a couple of awfully cranky bears on this island, but they were smart enough to respect the spear."

We paddled on. I shivered to think that we were going to attempt this crossing at night. "What about waiting for daylight?" I called over my shoulder. "I mean, you aren't really hiding anymore."

Silence was my answer. I should have known I was fingering a nerve. I was on my way home, but what in the world was he going to do now? Behind everything he said, even behind his laughter, there was sadness.

"How are you navigating?" I asked over my shoulder.

"By the current and the stars," he replied.

I took in the night sky, the half moon, the vague, dark shapes of the islands, the reflections of the moon and the stars on the water. I listened to the lapping of the waves on the drumlike sides of the skinboat and breathed the salt smell deep into my lungs. Eyes closed, I paddled on, stroke after stroke.

The explosive sounds of whales spouting on both sides of us took me back to how it all began, back at Cosmos Cove on Baranof Island. I kept paddling and let my mind go back to Hidden Falls, where I'd told my father I meant to carry on where he left off. I remembered all too vividly the windstorm that pushed me over to Admiralty, how I'd fought to stay upright. All the images came flooding through me: the brooding dark forests, that handful of devil's club spines, soaking rain and screaming eagles, the *tok-tok-tok* of ravens, the dead orca on the beach, gray and black wolves and a dog leading me through the clouds, a bear standing over me, a wild man running off with books in his hands and a startled look in his eyes.

I opened my eyes and found myself still on the water, still paddling, surrounded by dark islands and stars and sea, bobbing in a fragile boat over depths too cold and too deep even to think about.

Keep paddling. Don't ask. Have faith. Let it be.

**"J**UST KEEP PADDLING, WE'LL GET THERE."

The hoarse voice from the back of the boat snapped me back to the present. "Are we gaining on it?" I asked. "This strait seems so far across."

"This isn't a strait, it's Frederick Sound. Talk to me, keep me alert. Tell me about that part of the cave I've never seen."

"It's incredible—it has an underground stream," I began. I told about the salmon and the seals, about the bear leaving with a seal through the opening on the ridge above the cove.

"All this right under my nose!" he exclaimed. "Goes to show what I'd always expected. I had worlds more to learn about that island."

I asked why the salmon were running up through the cave when there was no gravel inside there, no place to spawn. After thinking it over, he guessed that the salmon were headed for the same lake as the salmon in the creek above ground, the one near his camp. The cave stream, he thought, must leave the lake underwater. The salmon swimming through the cave must use that opening to reach the spawning gravels on the bottom of the lake.

"Try this, then," I went on. "Would you believe caribou skulls in the cave, caribou antlers?"

"Sorry, that's flat-out impossible."

"I know, it sounds crazy. But my father found caribou bones in caves on Prince of Wales Island."

"Your father?"

"He was an archeologist, too."

"Aha," David Atkins said. "You're less and less a mystery. I assume your father had those caribou bones dated."

"He did. Along with bones from brown bears, marmots, a kind of tundra antelope. . . ."

"I can't believe this. That's less than a hundred miles south. All this from Prince of Wales Island?"

"All from Prince of Wales. And the dates showed that all those animals, and a lot more, lived on that island continuously for forty thousand years."

I heard only the sound of his paddle. I was so eager to hear his response, I barely registered on the blinking light from the buoy we were passing.

The silence went on so long, I broke it myself. "Really," I insisted. "He had the bones tested at the best lab in the country, at Boulder, Colorado."

"I know that lab. Used to use it myself. You're saying those animals were on these islands during the last forty thousand years? Archeologists have always believed that all these islands were covered with a thousand feet of ice, and that the ice sheets went all the way out to the continental shelf, right to the sea. We assumed that the brown bears swam here within the last ten thousand years, after the last Ice Age. That's just staggering to picture these islands ice-free. Nearly unbelievable."

"Not all the islands, just parts of some of them. The open parts of the islands would have been covered with tundra. There wouldn't have been many trees then."

"Similar to what you'd find around the Arctic Circle today."

"That's it. Good habitat for caribou, bears, salmon, all sorts of—"

"Did your father find any human remains?" The hermit-archeologist seemed to be caught between total disbelief—he was still wondering if I was making most of this up—and unbearable curiosity.

"One skeleton," I replied. "It's called Prince of Wales Man. Unfortunately, it was only nine thousand-and-some years old. He was hoping for something a whole lot older. You see, he never believed the standard stuff in the textbooks."

"What stuff? You mean he didn't believe that people used the land bridge across the Bering Strait from Siberia twelve thousand years ago? He didn't believe that's how the Clovis hunters came to the Americas?"

"Sure, he believed that, but he didn't believe they were *the first.*"

After a long pause, loaded with tension, Atkins said, "You're telling me that other people, earlier people, could have used all these islands as stepping-stones, something like that?"

He was beginning to imagine it. It was such a beautiful theory.

"From one stepping-stone to the next," I encouraged him. "Traveling by boat, hunting and fishing as they went, around the rim of the northern Pacific and down the west coasts of the Americas. And way before twelve thousand years ago. Who knows how long before?"

"That's a revolutionary idea," he said skeptically.

"I know, but listen to this. After my father made his discoveries on Prince of Wales, there was a huge discovery way down in Chile, in South America. A site with hundreds of artifacts that tested out to at least a thousand years older than the oldest Clovis artifacts ever found."

Again, silence. "David? Did you fall asleep on me?"

"I'm speechless."

"There's a site in Virginia called Cactus Hill that's *seventeen thousand* years old. Think how far back that pushes it."

The big man's amazement was strangled with a sudden cry. "On our right!" he yelled.

I turned and saw something that should never have been there. We'd been so deep in conversation we hadn't seen it coming—a gigantic ship, four or five decks high, lit up bright as a chandelier. I blinked and stared, trying not to believe what my eyes were telling me. In front of it there was no sound, none at all. "Is it heading our way?" I asked, hoping against hope that it wasn't.

"It sure is," Atkins replied.

The dog knew something was wrong. He stood up in the boat and yawned anxiously.

"Keep paddling," Atkins hollered.

"How do we know we aren't paddling into its path?"

"We don't. I can't tell yet."

I looked at the ship again. A cruise ship, steaming for Juneau in the middle of the night. And it was closing unbelievably fast.

I'm not going to get home after all, I thought. "Which way?" I yelled.

"There's a buoy ahead. It's at the edge of the shipping channel. We get close to it, the ship will pass behind us. Go! Paddle hard! Paddle as hard as you can!"

I put my head down and I paddled my lungs out. I paddled like there was no tomorrow, which was about to be the case. When I looked over my shoulder a few minutes later, the ship was still bearing down on us, but at an angle that would take it behind us. We were going to clear it. I let up.

"No!" the wild man roared. "Don't stop! Keep paddling! It's the wake that's the danger. We have to get as far away as we can. After it goes by, the wake is going to hit us like a tidal wave!"

Great, I thought, that's just great.

"I'm sorry," I heard him saying.

That was all I needed. It sounded like last words. I paddled like a banshee, sucking wind, breathing only terror. The ship was close now, a couple hundred yards away. It filled the sky.

The ship passed behind us. Then I heard the big man's paddle flailing. I looked and saw him backpaddling. "Help me spin it around!" he yelled. "We have to face the wave!"

I could see it all too well in the moonlight, the high lifting wave on the leading edge of the cruise ship's wake.

"Straight into it!" Atkins shouted. "Paddle straight into it as fast as we can!"

For a moment I wondered if he was right. I had my doubts about breaking through it. I could picture it pitching us end over end. But there was no time to turn and run. We were committed.

I paddled with everything I had. How I wished it was his weight in the front, not mine, at the moment we would meet the wave—which was going to be real soon.

At the crucial moment, with the wave high above us, I paddled one last stroke and then threw my weight onto the bow. We cleaved the top of the wave. The question was, did our skinboat have enough momentum to carry us through it? I felt a powerful surge from the stern— Atkins must have been paddling furiously—and then the wave broke on both sides of us as we pitched at a sickening angle, then came down upright.

"Bear!" Atkins yelled. I looked over my shoulder and realized that the dog was missing.

I STRUGGLED WITH MY PADDLE to meet a second wave. The wild man was no longer paddling, and it tossed us sideways. By dim moonlight, Atkins was trying to spot his black dog in the black water.

"There!" he cried finally. "Over there!"

I spotted the dog's blocky head, there one moment, gone the next. The Newfoundland was being sucked down into the powerful whirlpools in the cruise ship's wake.

"There," Atkins yelled again.

I spotted Bear and paddled hard. I maneuvered us close, and Atkins managed to haul the dog into the boat.

The big Newfie was beside himself with relief, whining and crying and beating his tail against the skinny wood frame on the floor of the boat, all at the same time.

I felt exactly the same way.

Atkins picked up his paddle. We continued on in silence. I was drained, weak all over, and angry, angrier by the minute. He could have gotten us both killed, and he wasn't going to say a thing. Finally I threw down my paddle and exploded. "Why did we have to do this in the dark?"

At first he didn't answer, then, "I've been hiding a long time."

"They already found you, don't you remember? Is it important that they don't catch you? Are you going to disappear again, is that it?"

"We would have been okay," he replied unconvincingly. "I got so excited about the archeology and all, I shut down the rest of my brain. I just wasn't paying attention. No excuse for it. I'm sorry, Andy."

It was the first time he'd called me by my name. I felt myself calming down. What did I care if he was going to play his hermit game for the rest of his life. I said, "All's well that ends well, eh?"

"Want to take up where we left off?" he suggested meekly.

"What do you mean?"

"We were talking about your father's theory, about the first people into the Americas moving south by boat, from island to island, during the Ice Age."

I said, "I'll talk about that any day."

"Hard to prove," he said as we paddled on. "Hard to find the evidence. Their camps would be under four hundred feet of seawater. Ocean level is much higher now, as I'm sure you know."

He was nibbling at my father's theory, but he wasn't really hooked yet. This wasn't trout fishing, where you set the hook; it was more like fishing for big channel cats. I needed to feed him some more bait, and let the big catfish hook himself. I said, "My father thought that the best chance for finding artifacts, or for burials, would be in caves. People could have climbed way above the sea and buried people inside caves, or left things."

"Like the ivory boat you showed me. That can be dated. Too bad there wasn't something more with it, especially bones."

I said, "There *were* bones, David." Then I told it all. I told about the burial and the two boat carvings I'd left untouched, and the little ivory effigies of sea mammals with tiny harpoons stuck in them. When I was done, Atkins didn't say anything for a long time, and then he said, "You've found something that might be monumentally big, depending on how the dates turn out. Your father would be proud. I have to ask . . . you speak of him in the past tense."

I told him about Baranof, what happened on Baranof Island, and then he said, "I would have liked to meet him."

Now he wanted to know all about me. I told him I was born in Eugene, Oregon, that my father was a professor at the university there. How after my father died, my mother moved us back to Colorado, where she was from. I told him about the orchard, how my mother and I lived just down the lane from my grandparents. I described living in the middle of ten acres of peach trees and apple trees, how my mother was a labor and delivery nurse, a "babyslinger," as she described herself.

"You have a fine life to go home to," he told me.

"What will you do now?" I couldn't help asking.

"I don't really know. I can't go back to Admiralty. That much is for sure."

He was going to let the conversation drop. There was something else I had to ask him. I wasn't very diplomatic; I just spit it out. "The newspapers reported that you drowned—that's what Shayla told me. Why did you want people to think you were dead?"

He shook back his huge mane of hair, then slowly smoothed down his long beard.

"You don't have to talk about it," I said.

"I'll give it a try," he said with an uncertain laugh. "I know I'm a strange one. . . . I figured I had to be presumed dead for my experiment to have any integrity. If I had people writing about what I was doing and coming to see me, it wouldn't."

"So you landed the boat, then put it in gear and sent it off trailing a fishing line?"

"No, I swam ashore. I just let the boat keep going without me."

"You're kidding. What did you have with you?"

"The clothes on my back, nothing else. I burned them as soon as I made some new ones. It was all a part of my experiment. I wanted to see if I could survive solely by prehistoric means. I wanted to see what it would actually be like to live in the Stone Age. I used to teach flint-knapping, fire starting and so on. I knew a lot of what I would need. At first it was only going to be for a year."

"But what about your family?"

"Not much family left. Both of my parents are gone. I never married."

"Why did you stay so long? Wouldn't a year be long enough?"

"The place grew on me. It happened so gradually I hardly noticed it at first."

He'd stopped paddling. I turned around to look at his scarred and weathered face. "Admiralty is one of the finest places left on earth," he said. "Nature still rules. I felt more alive there than I'd ever been. I came to feel like I was an explorer, living a big adventure."

"I understand about the adventure, but what do you mean by being an explorer?"

"I've been exploring the human past—the deep past. For 99 percent of human history we lived as a part of nature, not apart from nature. I wanted to know what that meant, what it felt like. I wanted to know who we were before all the technology, the cars, the big cities, before we became nature's lord and master. It was an idea that grew and grew until I had to act on it."

"What *does* it feel like?"

"That's just about impossible to explain in words. You can't tell where your skin leaves off and the universe begins, if that makes any sense to you."

"It doesn't, but I'll think about it. It just sounds too hard to me."

That got a laugh out of him. "Oh, I've always enjoyed doing things the hard way. I always was a low-tech guy. Never owned power tools, no microwave, no TV. Never even owned a car, but I did love my bicycle."

"I could never do what you did, not in a million years. Think of all you've been missing. . . ."

"Like shopping, waiting in lines, that kind of thing?" I could hear him chuckling.

"What about people? Didn't you miss having friends?"

"Sure. We're social by nature; it's hardwired into our brains. The first year was brutal. I had doubts I could stick it out mentally or physically. I lacked a shelter that provided storage. I lived hand-to-mouth, and it was rough. Then I found the dry camp under the big over-hang and was able to make myself comfortable. It was a challenge, making all those things you saw. I started thinking about staying. As time went by, I embraced the solitude. I came to see I wasn't alone at all. I had those books I discovered, and I had friends—they just didn't happen to be people."

"You mean the animals."

"Yes, and the island itself. Admiralty is so alive."

"I never knew there was any place like it."

*"Kootznoowoo,"* he said reverently. "The Fortress of the Bears."

The first light was dawning as silence seeped back in between us. It was Atkins who broke it after only a few minutes. "Those wildlife people are right, you know, about the dog needing to go. It's a marvelous thing that the wolves showed up. Admiralty is even wilder with wolves, and that's good."

"Where does that leave you and Bear?"

"I don't know. I just don't know. Start over again in the woods, I suppose. There are hundreds of islands, big and small. There's the mainland, the interior. We know how to take care of ourselves."

"But how? What will you do?"

"You're concerned about me, eh?"

"I am!"

"I really don't know. Haven't had enough time to figure it out yet. Maybe I could do something different. Maybe restore an old sailboat; I used to think about that. I always wanted to see the Queen Charlottes off the coast of B.C. I'd keep my eyes open. . . . Maybe I'd come across some more evidence to support your father's theory."

"You might really do that? Get a sailboat?"

A pause, and then, "No chance." His voice was thick with emotion.

"You lost me," I said, turning around. In the early light, his eyes were cloudy and confused.

"Everything I've told you is true, Andy, but it's not the whole truth."

"What are you talking about?"

"Maybe I stayed because I painted myself into a corner. Lost faith, dug myself in deeper and deeper."

"Lost faith in what?"

"The future. Our civilization is robbing it blind."

"That may be true," I said, "but vanishing doesn't help."

"I realize that," he agreed.

"You don't have to stay in the corner, you know. Why don't you walk out and do something?"

Suddenly I could see it, a way for him to reconnect. He was the one. "What about the cave on Admiralty? Couldn't you do the archeology? Someone will—why not you?"

"My credentials are a little rusty, Andy."

"Don't you want to find out how old the boats and bones in the cave are? What if they're twenty thousand, thirty thousand years old?"

"That would be the greatest find in American archeology."

"Well . . ."

"I'm too old for glory, Andy. It's not on my list."

"Not for glory, then. You'd have other good reasons. This is Admiralty we're talking about! You'd have a reason to stay on Admiralty!"

The rim of the sun was showing over the mountains of Kupreanof Island. He lapsed into gloom and quit talking. We paddled on.

The coast was looming, but before we reached it, a large gray powerboat raced out to meet us. The letters on the side of the vessel were bold and black. "U.S. Coast Guard!" I shouted.

The wild man's face was ashen. "This isn't how I pictured it," he said. "I thought I'd just drop you off and be gone."

"Someone on the cruise ship must have seen us."

The Coast Guard boat had cut its speed. The walking mountain range of a man was fenced in. The cutter was drawing close. There were four sailors at the rail. "Think of it as hitching a ride," I suggested.

"It's too fast, too selfish, too destructive, too scary," he said.

"What is?"

"The world."

"So, there's no hope for it?" I said bitterly.

I looked to the sailors and back to Atkins. His eyes were cloudy again, and he wasn't going to answer. As for me, I was so happy to see the Coast Guard, tears were streaming down my face. It was over.

# 24

THE SAILORS WERE AWFULLY HAPPY I was alive. My name had caused a lot of distress ever since I disappeared. They spared us from questions, maybe on account of David—his strange bark clothing, wildly overgrown hair, and grim look. He looked like a wild animal that had been captured and caged.

David wouldn't go inside. He sat on the deck with his arm around his dog. Bear was shivering with fear from all the strangeness. The din from the engines didn't help. I guzzled hot chocolate and went through almost a dozen donuts. After a ninety-minute ride we set foot on the Coast Guard dock at Kake.

The station commander came out to greet us. He reached out his hand and my feral friend took it. The commander introduced himself as normal as you please, like he was meeting somebody in a business suit. "David Atkins," the wild man said in return.

It wasn't long until we were both showered and dressed in Coast Guard–issue boxer shorts, trousers, and short-sleeved shirts. They even gave us our own bungalow. VISITING OFFICERS' QUARTERS the sign over the door said. Our windows looked out on boats in the harbor and rafts of hundreds and hundreds of logs. A totem pole soared a hundred feet or more above the village. The mountainsides were a checkerboard of logging clear-cuts, which reminded me how wild Admiralty really was. "This floor under my feet feels strange," I said to David. "It must feel really weird to you."

"Everything is weird," he acknowledged. "Don't worry about me and Bear. Run over to their office and make your calls."

Kake was wired into the rest of the world, with cell phones, e-mail, fax, and satellite. I called home and my grandmother answered. She sounded like she was next door.

Of course, my grandmother couldn't believe it was me. As soon as she caught her breath she told me that my mother was still in Juneau, had never left since she first went up there. I got the number for the Prospector Hotel, where she was staying. I gave my grandmother the Coast Guard number in Kake, then dialed up the Prospector Hotel as fast as I could.

My mother wasn't in, so I had to leave a message. Then I got Shayla Matlock's number and called her office. Bingo—it was Shayla on the other end. "Where are you?" was the first thing she said.

"Kake," I told her.

"How in the world did you get to Kake?"

"By skinboat, most of the way, with your hermit. The Coast Guard picked us up and brought us in."

"We were so sure you were still on Admiralty. Your mother is here in Angoon—got here this morning. I contacted her as soon as I could, to let her know you were alive. She was just over in Juneau."

"Can I talk to her?"

"She's at the chief's house, having coffee. I'll make sure you get to talk to her. Tell me, is David Atkins still with you?"

"You figured out his name," I said guardedly.

"I tracked down that old newspaper article. The main thing we've figured out is that we have egg on our face."

"What do you mean?"

"I mean, when the Forest Service guys found their way into that overhang where Atkins lived, they were astounded at all the artifacts, and a mural carved into the rock and . . . just everything. Couldn't get over it. They came back telling everybody that the place should be protected as one of Admiralty's historic sites, like the old Stan Price homestead on Pack Creek. Word has spread around the agencies like wildfire. The superintendent has signed on to the idea; he'd be the most unpopular guy in Alaska if he gave the hermit any more grief. Is Atkins okay?"

"I don't know if I'd use that word. He looks pretty disoriented."

"People want to know if he'd go back and live there as a sort of living exhibit. We could keep it very low key, just small groups of people coming to visit. What do you think?"

I couldn't imagine the wild man agreeing to that. It would be his worst nightmare. He'd be on display, no matter how low key they tried to make it. "I think I have a better idea," I said. "Just let me think about it some more. We can talk it over when I see you."

As soon as I got off the phone with Shayla I called Adventure Alaska in Sitka. Monica and Julia were out on another trip, but I left a message. It was a little confusing. The guy who answered the phone had just arrived from California and had no idea a kid from one of their trips was missing.

Nobody was home at Derek's or Darcy's. I had to talk to their answering machines. I was so disappointed, all I could spit out was that I was fine, happy to be alive, and would call as soon as I got home.

When we left Kake that afternoon, the Coast Guard flew us across Frederick Sound, over the mountains of Admiralty Island and into Angoon. That's where I met up with my mother, at the chief's house. My mother hugged me until I thought I'd stopped breathing. And she couldn't stop thanking David. He wasn't looking quite so wild anymore; he'd gotten a radical trim from the Coast Guard barber. Made him look a lot younger too. He turned out to be forty-nine.

Before Mom and I headed home, Shayla and David and I talked about finding a way for him to stay on Admiralty, a way that he could live with. He agreed he was interested in working on the archeology, but he wasn't about to be giving tours of his former camp, nothing like that. Finally Shayla suggested he could live in a small cabin, off by himself but near his old home. They'd work out the details later with the powers that be, but it would mean he couldn't keep his dog. Not if he was going to live on Admiralty.

It must have been agony, trying to make that decision. David slept on it and still didn't have an answer for Shayla in the morning. I had an idea he was going to ghost off into the wilderness somewhere with Bear. I didn't think I'd be around long enough to learn how it came out, but I was pessimistic. No matter what, he wasn't going to be parted from his dog.

The floatplane that would fly us to Juneau was splashing down, and we were all standing around the dock without a word to say. Shayla, my mother, and I sort of clustered together, with the wild man and Bear off to the side.

Bear would have come over and nuzzled my hand if I was by myself, but he was still shy as a wolf around strangers. I caught his eye, and mouthed the word good-bye, but couldn't stand to look David in the face. After all we'd put each other through, we might have been glad to get rid of each other, but I didn't feel that way at all. I wanted to know that he and his dog were going to be all right.

The pilot killed the motor and climbed out of his cockpit. He stepped from the pontoon onto the dock, where he tied off his airplane. "Two for Juneau?" he asked, looking around at the four of us.

My mother put her arm around my shoulder. "That would be Andy and me," she said cheerfully. I turned to the wild man with a lump the size of a basketball in my throat. "Well, I guess this is good-bye."

He reached out and put his huge hand on my shoulder.

"Maybe I won't see you soon, but this can't be good-bye."

I strained to decipher his words. "Does this mean you're rejoining the world?"

David glanced at the sprinkling of simple frame houses that was Angoon, and chuckled. "I got a couple of toes back in it, and it feels right."

To my surprise, his eyes were brimming and tears were about to spill. "Do me a favor, Andy?"

"Name it, big guy."

"Take Bear for your own. Take him back to Colorado. I have a hunch he'd thrive in your orchard. I want to do the archeology in our cave. I can handle it, and I want it real bad."

In a nanosecond, I ran it through in my head, about Bear. There was no reason it wouldn't work. I turned eagerly to my mother. She was already nodding her agreement. "You got a deal, and I got a dog," I told him. "I'll take good care of him."

Shayla's smile was dazzling. "Well, this is good news all the way around."

I was awfully attached to that ivory carving, but now was the time to give it up. That skinboat effigy would be a huge foot in the door for David. He could get hooked up with a university, I was sure of it, if he held the key to what might be a huge discovery. "Here's a start on your new beginning," I said, as I brought the ivory artifact out of its hiding place and pressed it into his hand.

Back home in Orchard Mesa, the most surprising thing happened. We started getting e-mail from David.

At first it was a stretch to picture him sitting in front of a computer. Then we began to hear from him almost every day, which was terrific. I guess that ancient boat and those ancient bones had set his imagination on fire, and he wanted to learn as much as he could as fast as he could. He had a lot of catching up to do, and the Internet turned out to be his ticket to ride. He could do it all without leaving the island.

By the end of August, David had accepted an assignment doing fieldwork on Admiralty for the University of Alaska in Juneau. He had a spot for his cabin all picked out, back in the trees near where the stream that ran by his old camp emptied into the sea. Pybus Bay was the name of the area, it turns out. He could live there as long as the archeology work lasted, which probably meant he could stay as long as he wanted. In addition to the burial chamber, there was that other room with all the animal bones, and the likelihood of even more discoveries.

In one of his e-mails, David mentioned that he hadn't made it to Juneau yet. Everything he needed, he said, he could find at the village store in Angoon. Somehow this didn't surprise me. Once the archeology work got started, his supplies would be flown in every couple of weeks by floatplane. He was going to have a laptop with a built-in antenna that would transmit right from Pybus Bay.

*As for my old camp*, David reported, *they had me put the rest of my things back right where they were, the ones I grabbed when we were leaving. They even retrieved the skinboat from Kake. It's going to the museum in Juneau. They'll display it as a replica without my name on it. I'm still jumpy about that sort of thing. They've closed off the overhang so nothing can be taken, and they've agreed not to do anything with it, or publicize it as a historic site, until I'm agreeable or dead. They think it will be of interest.*

*No kidding it will be of interest*, I e-mailed back. *Bet ya there's nothing like it anywhere. By the way, before they do an inventory or something, could you grab one of your Clovis points for me?*

*You got it*, he replied.

*Plus, I want flintknapping lessons*, I fired back.

*Got that too*, came his answer. *What else do you want?*

*I want to know how old Admiralty Island Man is.*

*You'll know as soon as I know. They're taking their sweet time at that lab there in Boulder. I hope he's old as the hills. Hey, Andy, notice that word, "hope"? I'm big on it these days, thanks to you. By the way, I'm adding people in boats to my mural—just off the coast of Alaska.*

Finally, the day came. It was in late fall. Bear and I were in the orchard. I had my back leaning against our oldest tree with my hand resting on the crown of Bear's head and I was thinking about Admiralty, how the snows in the mountains were forcing the deer down, how the wolves were following them into the forests, how the bears were going into hibernation, how David was starting the fieldwork.

The shadows in the orchard were long. The low autumn light was filtering golden through the trees. The fruit was all picked and the deer were coming into the orchard for the drops. Bear had amazing restraint. He'd perk up his ears at them, but never bark.

My mother came tearing through the orchard like the house was burning down. "News from Admiralty!" she cried, so loud my father might have heard. "Twenty-three thousand years old, Andy! Twenty-three *thousand* years!"

As soon as the news sank in, I realized this wasn't the end; it was just the beginning. So many islands, so many more caves waiting to be discovered. So many more clues to the puzzle of the earliest Americans. And I plan to be a part of it.

I know I'll have a lot more adventures in my life. But even if I live to be a hundred, I doubt one will ever come along to compare with those ten days on Admiralty. The beauty of the place, its raw power, live in my memory stronger than all the hardships. All I have to do is close my eyes and I'm back there hearing the spouting of the whales and the screaming of the eagles. I'm thankful that there is still such a place on this earth.

Admiralty, Kootznoowoo, the Fortress of the Bears. To this list of names I've added another. I'll always think of it as Wild Man Island.

# AUTHOR'S NOTE

*W*ild Man Island grew out of several sea kayak trips I took with my wife and paddling partner, Jean, along the shores of Admiralty and Chichagof Islands. Camping under the towering old-growth rain forest, observing brown bears at a salmon stream, and paddling among sea otters, harbor seals, Steller's sea lions, and breaching humpback whales gave me a wealth of impressions and the desire to write a story that would invite readers into the island world of southeast Alaska.

During the 1990s I had been following the revolutionary discoveries in American archeology regarding when and how the Americas were peopled. Some of the most exciting developments were coming from caves on Prince of Wales Island, in southeast Alaska. Dr. Timothy Heaton's excavations there uncovered a continuous record of bear, caribou, and other animal remains going back at least forty thousand years— throughout the last Ice Age, which previously was thought to have precluded the possibility of human coastal migrations. Archeologists were astounded by the implications, and so was I. If bears and caribou had survived there, then so might have humans.

As of now, the oldest evidence of humans in southeast Alaska, on Prince of Wales and other islands, is dated to around ten thousand years ago. There is good reason to believe that new discoveries will push this date back, perhaps much farther back. I began to think about writing a story in which a character makes a discovery that does just that. A cave would be the most likely place for him to make such a find. I could draw on my caving experiences in Missouri and New Mexico, and on Vancouver Island, British Columbia.

Admiralty Island, with its wilderness quality, promised the ideal setting. Its timeless old-growth forests suggested hidden secrets. I asked Jim Baichtal, a geologist with the U.S. Forest Service in Juneau, if karst formations (cave-bearing limestone) had been mapped on Admiralty. Yes indeed, he replied, and named several locales, including the Pybus Bay area, which are rich in karst but unexplored as yet for caves. This situation suited my fictional purposes perfectly. That the Pybus Bay area was one of the ice-free refugia in southeast Alaska during the Ice Age, and home to caribou and brown bears, is speculation on my part. The human remains found in my story and the date attached to them are fictional as well.

The factor that clinched Admiralty as my setting was some surprising news published by Friends of Admiralty Island in their Winter 2000 newsletter. A U.S. Fish and Wildlife Service biologist had observed what almost certainly was a wolf, along with a feral dog, at a hunter-killed bear carcass. The two were exhibiting courtship behavior, which alarmed the biologist. If a small pack of wolves had swum from the mainland, they would have a profound effect on the ecology of the island, but interbreeding with dogs would jeopardize their integrity as wild animals. I could picture wolves as a factor in the novel, and the dog becoming a catalyst in the plot.

In addition to Jim Baichtal, I would like to thank Terry Fifield, an archeologist for the U.S. Forest Service on Prince of Wales Island, and Ed Grossman, a wildlife biologist with the U.S. Fish and Wildlife Service in Juneau, for their generous assistance.

All characters in this novel are entirely fictional.

For further reading, I would point interested readers to "Hunt for the First Americans," by Michael Parfit, *National Geographic*, December 2000; to *Bones, Boats, and Bison: Archeology and the First Colonization of Western North America*, by E. James Dixon, University of New Mexico Press, 1999; and to Timothy Heaton's website www.usd.edu/~theaton/alaska, for "The Fossil Gold Mine in the Caves of Southeast Alaska" and other articles and links.

The ecology of salmon, seals, and brown bears in the cave stream described in *Wild Man Island* is based on an actual cave stream on Chichagof Island that flows out of Kook Lake. The abandoned cannery in this story, in a cove on the southern end of the island, is an actual place called Tyee, a tiny fishing port and cannery that shut down in the mid-1950s. Earlier in the twentieth century it had been a whaling station.

Admiralty Island was long the target of large-scale logging. Around 90 percent of the island—nearly a million acres—was spared that fate when President Jimmy

Carter signed a bill that gave it national monument status in 1978. Let's hope that a thousand years from now, it will still be one of the wildest places on earth, still the Fortress of the Bears.

Durango, Colorado
April 2001